GURGLEWOBBLERS
The Quest for the Jewelled Egg

GURGLEWOBBLERS

The Quest for the Jewelled Egg

CHUCK DICKENS

Matador
9 Priory Business Park,
Wistow Road
Kibworth Beauchamp
Leicester LE8 0RX, UK
Tel: (+44) 116 279 2299
Fax: (+44) 116 279 2277
Email: books@troubador.co.uk
Web: www.troubador.co.uk/matador

ISBN 978 1780880 235

British Library Cataloguing in Publication Data.
A catalogue record for this book is available from the British Library.

Typeset in 12pt Book Antiqua by Troubador Publishing Ltd, Leicester, UK

Matador is an imprint of Troubador Publishing Ltd

Printed and bound in the UK by TJ International, Padstow, Cornwall

To all children around the world

CONTENTS

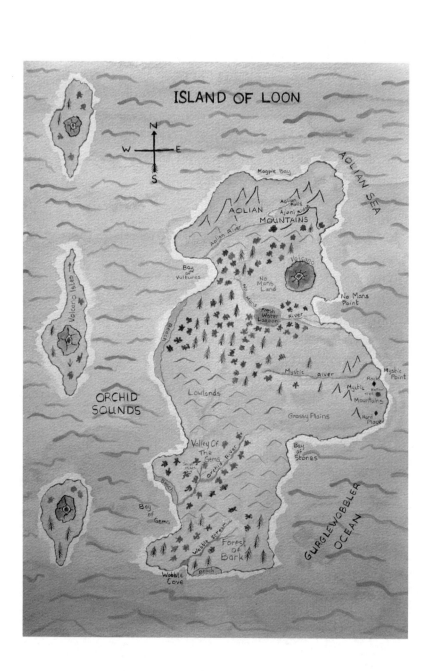

CHARACTER NAMES AND MEANINGS

THE GURGLEWOBBLERS

HUGO (twin 1) – English-Fire.
GUY (twin 2) – English-Guide.
LIVIA – English-The Olive.
SETH – English-The Appointed One.
LEO – English-Bold Lion.
TALIA – English-Blooming.

THE ORCHIDS

KIANDRA- English-Magical Water Baby.
GENERAL JOE- English- From Joseph.
RAFE- English-From Ralph.
DARVA-Slavic-Honeybee.
ARTIE (twin 1)-English- From Arthur.
BANJO (twin 2)-English-Musical Instrument.
LUELLA-English-Warrior.
KOHANA-Japanese-Little Flower.
GAZALI-African-Mystic.

THE FLOWER PEOPLE

1. ZENA – Greek-Hospitable.
2. ROXY – English-Rosy.
3. ELIE – English-From Eleanor.

THE VULTURE

AJANI – African-He Who Wins.

THE THIEVING MAGPIES

1. CEDRIC – English-Chief.
2. BOYCE – German-From the Woods.
3. BUZZ – Gaelic-In the Woods.
4. CHAD – English-Battle Warrior.
5. JALEN (the rookie) – English-Bird of Light.

CHAPTER 1

ARTIE MEETS CEDRIC IN THE FOREST

Near the bottom of the world in the Tropic of Lantartica lies the secret Island of Loon. The roar from the Aolian Falls to the north echoes through the vast landscape. As the river meanders through the Aolian Mountains down to the Bay of Vultures, it becomes a distant whisper to an eager ear. The mountains breathe a misty condensation, bringing a sweet tropical breeze that casually swims through the air before diving down the back of the throat.

In the summer the island boasts a pastel dawn, followed by a magnificent florescent dusk that creeps behind the islands highest point of the mountains.

One fine morning Cedric the magpie had gone out for his constitutional. Dressed in his green tie, turned up short trousers, and gold adornments he cut a dashing figure. He had left the mountains at the crack of sparrow's kneecaps, and flown south from Ajani Ridge. As Cedric flew over No Mans Land he saw vibrant magma spewing out from the raging volcano towards the Aolian Sea, and was glad to leave this harsh landscape behind him and reach Fresh Water Lagoon. Cedric was gliding high on the thermals and looked down to see the water refracting the sparkling colours of topaz and pearl, gently shimmering in the half-light.

This utopian theatre emulates a gratifying aromatic blend of larch, pine and lavender amongst the copious quantities of deciduous forest and fertile pasture. Cedric found the air was much more refreshing here as it created a place of sensuous tranquility. It was just after sunrise when he arrived at the edge of The Valley of the Gems where the Orchid and Flower people reside, and is no place for a magpie, especially Cedric.

Back home on Ajani Ridge Cedric is responsible for supplies of food scraps to the thieving magpie clan that he presides over, and keeping the barrel of Adams Ale (water) topped up to the brim at the back of their cave. This was an easy task for Cedric, because the bamboo gully flowed directly from the Aolian Falls into the cave. All magpies are clever but sly creatures; they are always out for their own, but more often than not, keep a watchful eye on one another.

* * *

As the shadows of the clouds drew back across the valley, Cedric was perched high up amongst the trees. He witnessed these early morning ghostly shapes imitating shimmering fishes swimming across the landscape. His black cowboy hat adorned with a red ruby stud was angled over his eyes. He watched the dry ground that had itself become a victim of the amethyst ultra violet rays and lay in wait for any gullible victim, so he could trick them any which way that was possible. From Cedric's viewpoint a whirlpool of thoughts ran through his mind. "I must not fail or disappoint my master, Ajani. I must fulfil my mission and return with a treasure as promised."

Cedric's mind soon began to switch to thoughts of his

favourite scraps, a large platter of crocodile entrails. He licked his lips and smacked his bill together. Cedric was relaxing while absorbing the evenly pitched clicking sounds trapped within the trees. It reminded him of an orchestra and was music to his ears.

Suddenly, just as the warm haze of the sun was sending Cedric to sleep, the jingle jangle of his gold rings and bracelets broke his sedative state as the biggest horse-chestnut struck the branch as it plummeted to the ground. The solid *boom* finale was followed by the crunch of the foliage, catching Cedric's attention immediately. Again he quickly reassured himself. "I must not fail," he whispered with an air of confidence.

Skipping down Gem trail on the edge of the valley was a baby bee orchid humming a soulful melody. He instantly came to a halt, and was distracted by the green and red shimmering shell of a four-eyed shickleback. The shickleback is one of the shyest of Loons insects. He stretched out his yellow hairy hand to stroke it, because he loved all animals and insects. Carefully studying the ground beneath his feet, the bee orchid could not see Cedric tucked away.

"Hello there little fella," said Cedric from his branch.

Startled, the bee orchid looked up and caught a glimpse of the ruby on Cedric's hat. "Hello, who are you?" he replied.

"I'm Cedric. I come from the mountains of the north, where I live with my friends, and I am a collector of sparkling treasures. Have you got anything nice and shiny with you?"

"No, not today," the orchid replied, as he continued to be distracted by the ruby.

As the conversation carried on the baby bee orchid introduced himself as Artie, and explained that he had

3

woken very early this morning before the pastel dawn. Before long Artie started to talk about where he lived and that he was the identical twin brother of Banjo.

"My brother Banjo is very clever, he can play the musical instrument named after himself, and I can beat an Irish drum like you have never heard."

"Oh, is that so Artie! But I'm more interested in other things, especially if they are gold and sparkle," retorted Cedric.

The bee orchids lived with their mother Darva on her stem in the valley. They both had the unique ability to be able to detach themselves from her to go on walkabouts, but they always made sure they returned home for bedtime. If they were more than twenty claps late they would miss out on their mother's home made hot pollen juice, which was always gulped down before a night time story of barricades, bushes and battles. She would then wrap them up in their mauve petals to keep the cool evening moisture from their delicate little red bodies, like a snug warm blanket.

Artie rambled on to Cedric that he and Banjo preferred the juice lukewarm as they would compete to see who could drink it the fastest, and he had won the last sixty times.

"Not that I was counting or anything," Artie justified, as he continued to declare his own knowledge of Loon. He told Cedric that near Wobble Cove in the Forest of Bark live the Gurglewobblers, and they are the guardians of a treasured jewelled egg designed by Cabbergé eons ago.

The Gurglewobblers are six little friends who are very short in height with large heads, big eyes, and wide mouths. Artie picked up a twig and etched in the dust to describe to Cedric what they look like.

"They have big ears like this, see, and large wobbly

bottoms like this," Artie said.

"So Artie, tell me more about this treasured jewelled egg," asked Cedric, as he glided down from his branch to perch on a sandy coloured rock.

"I don't know everything," Artie said innocently while scratching his hand on the grassy ground.

"All I know is that there is an Elder called Seth who guards it and he is one of the Gurglewobblers in the Forest of Bark, they live in tree houses, and his is the one with the purple door. I was listening from behind a bush and heard them say that the treasured jewel is egg shaped, and is a glistening beauty inlaid with rubies and bands of gold that crisscross the turquoise enamel. I overheard mum talking to our queen about it, and that's how I know," said Artie.

Artie had caught Cedric's attention. Cedric's eyes lit up, he was now very intrigued.

"You have done very well Artie. You shall be rewarded, and now I must return to the north. You must not tell anybody what you have told me or that we have met, or there will be no reward. Now promise me that you will do as I ask," Cedric said, looking Artie straight in the eye with a menacing expression across his face.

"Okay, I promise," Artie retorted nervously, as Cedric flew away, northbound.

In his heart Artie knew he had made a terrible mistake by talking to Cedric, but the promise of a reward helped him to ease his own conscience. He thought to himself that he could only hope that his reward would be worthwhile. Could it be a pearl or a special key? he mused. Could it be a new catapult to play with, after all, he accidentally snapped his last summer when playing with Banjo. He continued to question himself as to what it might be, but had never actually thought to ask.

5

The Forest of Bark

Artie said goodbye to the shy shelled shickleback, and continued to carry on wandering around in the forest, still thinking about his brief encounter with Cedric. His stomach soon began to rumble when he became hungry, and decided it was as good a time as any to head for home to the safe haven of his family. When he arrived back in the Valley of the Gems, he kept his promise and never mentioned his meeting with Cedric to anyone.

* * *

Much further south on the island is the Forest of Bark where the Gurglewobblers reside. The northern part of Loon remains a mystery to the six little friends. When the island's autumn rainstorms arrive, it carries with it the scent of acrid sulphur from the north, which is a sure sign of the seasonal change.

The identical twins Hugo and Guy are two courageous and strong Gurglewobblers. Together they make a dynamic duo with their practical jokes, enthusiasm for life and acrobatics, which they regularly practiced from the long dangling rope that hangs from the trunk of Hugo's tree house.

They both chose to dress the same, white t-shirts, braces, black diamond studded chokers, which were ancestral hand me downs, and black boots. Hugo wears green jeans and Guy wears dark crimson jeans, and both of them wear an earring in their left ear. Hugo's reddish brown hair has been shaved both sides leaving a tuft in the middle, and Guy's is spiky all over just like a hedgehog.

Both Guy and Hugo enjoy the freedom of fishing from their motor launch, *Moana*, when translated means *ocean*. When they go off exploring together they can get up to all sorts of antics without being under any watchful eyes.

Seth the Elder is the oldest by some ten thousand years, and so the more mature, and he argues the wisest of the group. He is *thee* custodian of the jewelled egg which has kept them all alive and in perfect health for many centuries, and is fearless to the happenings in the north.

Seth doesn't like to be without his blue hat with the black peak that he aptly calls his 'thinking cap.' He has short brown hair, wears a white collarless shirt with a red tie and blue dungarees. From his tree house every morning after he has sipped his warm nettle and honey tea, he ensures his shoes are polished to perfection, "You can tell a lot about a fellow's character from his shoes," he often remarked to Livia.

Livia, being the playful one of the friends usually replied with a tease, "Well that makes Hugo a dirty old boot then!" she retorted whilst looking at Austen her blue and red parrot sitting on his perch by her door. Then Livia blew a cheeky kiss in the direction of a frowning Hugo. Her beaming smile lights up any tree house. No Gurglewobbler stays displeased with Livia for very long.

Livia dresses herself in yellow dungarees with white flower shaped buttons that compliment her white t-shirt. She never goes anywhere without her red ribbons in her orangey yellow hair. Grandma Gurgle had always told her that as well as being handy for tying crops, a red ribbon brings good luck in friendship, so she always wore two red ribbons for double luck.

Skeptical of Livia's superstitions is the self-confessed realist Leo. He strongly believes that a Gurglewobbler makes his own luck through correctly nurturing nature. The fresh water stream that flows through the Forest of Bark and on to Wobble Cove, ensures enough nutrients for the Gurglewobblers to harvest a flourishing crop to be enjoyed by all at every meal. Leo has brown hair and wears a grey trilby hat to protect his head from the rays of the sun as he harvests. A white handkerchief tucked in to the top pocket of his blue waistcoat, allows him to dab away droplets of sweat from his brow after working the land with his hoe. His red trousers and tie compliment his long sleeved white shirt with mud stained cuffs.

Leo's vegetable patch and herb garden are a wealthy spectrum of rich greens and copper browns, that craft an earthy patchwork as they grow in harmony alongside Seth's sisal plants and beehives. The smell of moist potatoes, mint and honey inject the night air with delicious aromas that are met with approval by each Gurglewobbler as they sleep in their tree houses at night.

Each tree house has a different coloured stable door with matching window shutters. A nightlight above each door ensures enough illumination for Hugo and Guy to play their favourite nighttime prank of knock down ginger.

Talia is frequently woken by Hugo and Guy's midnight mischief. Feeling restless she would light the candle Hugo had made for her as an April fool, from the thick glucky liquid extracted from the seaweed off the beach. She would gently play with her long black hair, which was always parted in the middle. One half is combed straight, and the other half is a mass of curls that dangle like corkscrews to show off her earring. Day or night Talia can be seen in blue jeans, a red waistcoat and a white collarless shirt with her sleeves rolled up to her elbows. She often enjoyed spending her evenings daydreaming out of her window while talking to her cuckoo named Pink's, about what might lurk north of the Forest of Bark.

CHAPTER 2

THEFT OF THE JEWELLED EGG

On the highest peaks of the rocky Aolian Mountains is the cave that has been taken over by Ajani and his thieving magpie warriors. From Ajani Ridge there is a spectacular panoramic vista from the rocky crag right across Orchid Sounds to the distant uninhabited smaller volcanic islands. From here Ajani and the thieving magpies could hear the sounds of the waves crashing like thunder against the seashore, releasing a fresh salty aroma of sea air into the atmosphere, though it was not always enough to mask the stench from the rotting carcasses on top of the ridge.

The evil vulture Ajani resides on the ridge, which he has named after himself, a symbol of his own self-importance. He is a kleptomaniac who originated from the mountains of Arcifa decades ago, and lives alongside his five magpie warrior servants, Cedric, Boyce, Chad and Buzz, and most importantly the rookie magpie Jalen who is the trainee of the group.

Ajani ruled by fear with a temperament to match, and any defiance from his thieving magpies would be catastrophic for them. His neck is scrawny and long, his eyes cruel and dark like giant black rubies. His black baseball cap is worn back to front, covering the bald patch on the back of his head. With his lethal long sharp hooked bill, lean brown body and large blue wings that span six feet across, he makes for a vicious unyielding force to be reckoned with.

* * *

Boyce was lounging around at the mouth of the cave that they called home. He was keeping a beady eye out for Cedric's return, and was curious to know where he might have been. The patch that covered his right eye was purely for show, as he had always fancied himself as a pirate. Like all his buddy magpies he was green, blue, black and white in colour. The feathers on is head stood erect and he never went anywhere without his green handkershute, which is a cross between a tiny handkerchief and a parachute. Boyce acquired it some years ago on a private deal with his Uncle Swagg, a now deceased relative. Uncle Swagg had always warned Boyce to 'be prepared', a lesson which he would later forget.

Buzz strolled over to join Boyce at the mouth of the cave as he could tell Boyce was becoming agitated.

"Don't you know that curiosity killed the cat, eh Boyce?" Buzz remarked.

"Yes Buzz, but I'm a bird," said Boyce, "so that's okay."

They were contemplating what Cedric might bring back with him, another emerald necklace perhaps, a pair of sunglasses, or even a watch of some description?

Buzz had had enough of the musty stale aromas that came from within the cave, and chatting with Boyce was a nice distraction as they stood together shooting the breeze.

Buzz wore his straight hair parted in the middle resembling the pages of an open book. His eyes are shifty and he is slightly taller than his companions, and can be terribly accident prone. He is good at arithmetic and has a good sense of humour. Buzz would insist on taking his infra-red night vision goggles with him on all expeditions, they had been a rare gift from Boyce from one of his former deals, so Buzz treasured them.

Chad was busy collecting old broken bones and cutting more twigs and different sized branches to replace the rotten untidy ones in Ajani's nest. The stench from the rancid carcasses near his master's scruffy pile were attracting the bugs and pesking Chad beyond belief, buzzing in his face and trying to land on his beak. He fought a constant losing battle with these Loonatics and was impatient to finish this undesirable task, while having to constantly keep brushing them aside with his wings.

Chad is the muscles of the group, and he adorns himself with red ruby studded gold amulets that can also be used for cutting wood, with its sharp blades attached to the sides. He is amazingly strong and has well formed biceps. Just the look of him with his mohican hairstyle and sweat band was enough to put fear into any opponents heart. His most useful and prized possession was his crowbar. It was made of semi-precious metal, converted from a paperclip that he had found washed up on the beach last summer. Chad had acquired many magnificent skills over the years. He had learnt to split his tail in two and still be able to fly. To entertain and impress his chums, he liked to show off by skateboarding up and down the walls of the cave.

* * *

The early morning pastel coloured mist that had hung over the Aolian Mountains had now dissipated, allowing the sweeter aromas from the vegetation below the rocky crag, to help counteract the stink from the scraps of rotting flesh and old broken discarded animal bones that lay around on Ajani Ridge.

Boyce and Buzz spotted Cedric high on the thermals, fast approaching and coming into land. They were glad to have him firmly back on home territory, but strangely enough he appeared to be empty handed.

Upon Cedric's return from the Lowlands on the edge of the Valley of the Gems, he strutted straight passed Boyce and Buzz as though they didn't exist. Cedric's expression upon his face was one of seriousness as he went directly to report to his leader Ajani. Cedric informed him of his meeting in the forest with the baby bee orchid Artie, and the existence of a jewelled egg that is protected by a small race of people in the south, called the Gurglewobblers.

Ajani listened intently to Cedric's story. His big black ruby eyes wide open with exhilaration, and he wanted this jewel in his possession, "I want this prize. He who dares! Wins!" Ajani said.

Ajani gave Cedric strict instructions to come up with a strategy to steal this precious cargo to add to his collection of treasures that he had accrued over decades. Ajani had a stunning collection of jewellery and a fabulous gold fob watch that had been found by Chad on the beach at the Bay of Vultures some years earlier. And so Ajani's plan to steal the jewelled egg was hatched.

* * *

The amount of natural sunlight beaming through the entrance of the stinking dank dark cave was just enough to enable Cedric to see what he was doing. He sat on his broken wooden chair at his matching wooden desk made of old cast off planks, studying his shabby maps. He had made a plan to steal this jewelled egg, he knew the location and thought to himself, "This will be very easy."

Pausing for a moment, Cedric nibbled on some red fruit berries that lay on the table. As he popped one after the other into his mouth, the skins burst open on his tongue exploding with juicy tartness like a carbonated lotion, catching the back of his throat as they slid down.

Cedric was enjoying this moment of peaceful tranquility as he glanced behind him to take a sneaky peek at the luminescent sunset refracting off the sea. It was like an advancing orange and red carpet of rich inviting colours. In the distance he could hear the crashing waves against the seashore, bringing with it seaweed and other memorabilia washed up from the ocean floor.

"The beach shall provide slim pickings compared to this deal," Cedric said to himself, turning back to glance at his maps. "We shall wait until nightfall, my plan is, oh, so simple."

The idea was to fly to the Forest of Bark, slip in through the window, harness the egg and fly out with it.

"They can't possibly get this wrong!" said Cedric.

Cedric called Boyce over to the where he was seated, and asked him to go and round up Buzz and Chad inside the cave.

The rookie magpie Jalen was still fast asleep and was too young to be a jewel thief. He was only a few weeks old when his mother had died. Chad had found him abandoned in the forest on one of their expeditions, and brought him back to the mountains with him for training purposes.

"This baby will be our future," Chad muttered,

cradling him carefully with both wings.

The inside of their cave was musty, cold and damp with a dirt floor. The walls were high and sparsely decorated. Apart from Cedric's table and chair there was only a small cracked mirror, which hung on the wall just inside the cave entrance, guaranteed to bring them all bad luck for seven years. Cedric had gouged seven marks into the wall to mark the years, of which two had been crossed out, leaving five years left to go.

Jalen slept in the nursery quarters where he was allowed to keep a large toy box for his amusement, but really it had been cleverly disguised as training equipment.

All the thieving magpies slept in hammocks and fed on scraps from Ajani, who for the most part was usually found outside brooding on his nest. He had been known on occasions to stick his beak inside the cave entrance to keep a check on his jewel thieves, making sure they were doing exactly as he had ordered.

Over time Ajani had become bone idle. Why should he be bothered to fly around hunting for food or scouring the landscape for jewels, when he had his servants to do all the work for him? In his mind they were lucky to have him as their leader.

Finally Buzz, Boyce and Chad arrived inside the cave.

"Now gather round the table boys, it looks like tonight is thee night," said Cedric, as they all shuffled over.

"Thee night for what?" asked Buzz, looking worried, as he gave Cedric a skeptical glance. After all Cedric had made some wacky plans in the past.

"Well, if you would just keep quiet, all shall be revealed," answered Cedric impatiently, and began to explain.

"I have spent much of the day with our leader Ajani, who has given me specific instructions to make a strategic plan to steal an egg from a group of people called the Gurglewobblers. These subordinates reside in the Forest of Bark at the most southerly point of our island." There was a moment of silence. Cedric continued, "I have devised a plan," he said.

Chad was anxious to get started, "Come on, spill the beans," he retorted tiresomely.

"Okay, okay, keep your feathers on," Cedric replied, sucking one of his fruit berries, nearly gagging from the tartness as he swallowed it.

"Cut to the chase," said Boyce. "We don't have all night!"

"That's where your wrong Boyce!" said Cedric gleefully, rubbing his wing tips together at the prospect, and dribbling fruit berry juice from his beak down his green tie. "We do have all night, and it's tonight. There will be a full moon, so the theft of this cargo should be a piece of cake."

"Uh!" they all said together sounding surprised.

"Cake, did you say piece of cake?" Buzz asked, jumping up and down with excitement, "I haven't had cake for ages." He was casting his mind back to last spring when he found a huge piece of fudge cake that stood like a giant boulder on the beach that was bursting out at the seams with butter fudge filling, and crawling with Loonatics all over the gritty sand, "That was a square meal, two of my five a day!" he declared.

Chad looked at Buzz with contempt, rolling his eyes to the sky, "Not that sort of cake, featherbrain, you know, piece of cake, easy job and all that."

"Oh!" said Buzz, feeling rather disappointed, "that sort of cake!"

Cedric turned away from Buzz and carried on showing his chums the map, and explained the most direct route for them to take, then continued, "Chad, you will fly in first. The tree house that you are looking for has a purple door. This is where the Elder Seth lives. He is the guardian of the egg."

Chad interrupted Cedric, "An egg, what do we want with an egg? Are we going to hatch it or something?"

"Oh, do be quiet Chad," barked Cedric, "It is no ordinary egg, nincompoop! It was hand-made many centuries ago by the craftsman Cabbergé. It is very valuable, festooned with rich jewels and gold."

Suddenly Buzz, Chad and Boyce's eyes lit up with delight.

Chad spoke with enthusiasm, "That sounds more like it!"

"Back to the plan," continued Cedric, as he struck a match against the stone support for the table and lit his candle. "Chad, when you get to the tree house, you will probably have to force the window open. The Elder Seth sleeps with the shutters down. Once it has been opened, Boyce will fly in with his handkershute, grab the egg, strap the cargo to his back and fly back out of the window."

"So what do I do?" asked Buzz.

"You're the look out, and if anyone wakes up, your job will be to cause a diversion," replied Cedric.

"I'm okay with that," said Buzz with a smirk across his face, and feeling confident that he could cope with this mammoth task, "mm! I mustn't forget my infra-red night vision goggles."

"So, are we all set to go boys?" asked Cedric.

"Yes," they all answered in unison.

"We will rendezvous here at mid-night, so get

something to eat and have forty winks, it's a long flight. E.T.A. 4.15 a.m," said Cedric, "Just before sunrise."

Buzz, Boyce and Chad left Cedric alone in the cave in the candlelight and went to find some scraps to eat and Adams Ale to drink from the rear of the cave. They retired to their hammocks to rest, as they were going to need all their energy to get them through *this* night.

* * *

The magpies were rested, fed and watered and ready for action. It was now time to rendezvous with Cedric.

Boyce strapped his handkershute on to his back and put on his eye patch, he always wore it whether he needed to or not.

Chad put on his gold ruby studded amulets and flexed his muscles, turning this way and that. He stood admiring his physique in the broken cracked mirror on the wall to make sure he looked swell. Chad picked up his precious metal crowbar and placed it in between his amulet and the feathers on his right wing.

Buzz leapt out of his hammock and pronounced himself fit for purpose as he was. "What you see is what you get!" he announced out loud to whoever was listening, which was nobody.

Cedric had entrusted them all with such an important task, but considered it so straightforward that it was unnecessary for him to attend on this particular mission.

Zero hour had arrived. The magpies were fully equipped with everything that they needed for the task that lay ahead of them. Cedric calculated that their flight should take them around four hours if there were no hitches.

Chad, Boyce and Buzz took off from the flat shelf of

Ajani Ridge, swooping down above the treetops between the foothills at the base of the mountain in a southerly direction. The gentle breeze of this warm balmy night was perfect. The stars in the sky sparkled like a billion diamonds against a backdrop of silky smooth black velvet. The large full moon shone as bright as the biggest silver medallion you ever saw, illuminating the sky, silhouetting the outline of the landscape below them.

So far everything appeared to be going according to Cedric's plan.

As the trio flew over No Man's Land, deliberately by-passing the live volcano in the east that was still spewing magma, they could not help but inhale a breath of the wafting acrid sulphur air. As it meandered its way down their gullets, it felt like a thousand sharp knives cutting deep within when it reached their tiny lungs, and made their eyes stream like a waterfall. They were glad to leave this toxic gas behind them as they approached the utopian landscape of Fresh Water Lagoon. Here, the air was wonderfully more oxygenated. Breathing easy again the magpies continued on over the Lowlands past the Bay of Stones, to arrive at their destination in the Forest of Bark precisely on time, just before the dawn chorus.

As they approached their target, Chad saw the purple door that Cedric had told him about. The band of thieves proceeded to land one by one on a thin ragged branch of a tree nearby. The gentle movement of the leaves on the trees blowing in the breeze, drowned out the sound of the trickling water from the stream that shimmered in the moonlight.

The magpie warriors silently tiptoed along the serrated branch to the far end for a better viewpoint, almost nudging each other off along the way.

Buzz was looking all around him at this exciting new

environment, and not looking where he was meant to be going. He tripped on a protruding notch of wood and fell over, having to flap his wings rapidly up and down to correct his balance, squawking loudly.

"Oh, do be quiet Buzz," Chad whispered abruptly.

"You'll wake everybody up. Look over there," Chad added, pointing to the cuckoo and parrot asleep on their perches, "nobody told us about them, we will have to be exceedingly quiet now."

"I forgot my infra-red night vision goggles Chad," said Buzz sheepishly, gazing all around him at this magical place that he had never been to before.

The early morning dew twinkled like ice crystals on the lush green grass below, producing a fragrance from the herbs and vegetation that was aromatically delicious, and much more pleasantly refreshing than the stench of their own surroundings back home.

"This is typical of you Buzz, you have got a bird's eye view from here, so you should not have too much bother," retorted Chad.

Chad then turned to Buzz and asked, "What are you going to do for a diversion if it arises?"

"Ooh, I'll think of something spontaneously." Buzz replied, staring at Chad.

"You mean you don't have a plan?" interrupted Boyce feeling somewhat exasperated as he mopped the sweat from his brow with the tip of his wing.

"Erh, well, not exactly, I'll just flap my wings and squawk loudly. I can think on my talons you know," said Buzz nonchalantly, looking skyward observing the Milky Way from where his pals were stationed.

"Here's hoping," said Boyce, whispering into Chad's ear while looking in the opposite direction to where Buzz was perched.

"What's that Boyce? Speak up when you mumble," retorted Buzz sharply.

"Nothing Buzz," answered Boyce.

"Are we all ready?" asked Chad.

"Ready and waiting," replied Boyce and Buzz in unison with an eager anticipation.

Chad was focusing on his mission at hand. He swooped forwards to the overhanging grey sandstone windowsill, making sure not to disturb these birds from their slumber, bypassing Talia's tiny pale green cuckoo.

"Coo, look at him over there, what a smooth joker he is, in his coat of many colours!" said Chad, referring to Austen, Livia's red and blue parrot.

"My, my, these are big trees, bigger, wider and sturdier than I expected!" Chad said to himself, as he tried to open the purple shutters, but they were utterly and completely firmly jammed.

"Where's my crow bar?" said Chad quietly to himself in a whisper, "ah, here it is." He pulled it out from between his amulet and the feathers on his wing and tried to force the first window shutter open. It would not budge, so Chad tried the other. By now his crowbar had bent in two, taking on the appearance of a hairpin, it was stuck hard. He flew back down to terra firma and placed his bent crowbar gently on to the ground in the wet grass.

"I'll need to use my blade for this job," Chad mused.

His amulet had a razor sharp blade on the edge of it, so Chad flew back up to the windowsill feeling the cool sandstone under his claws, and proceeded to cut around the outer perimeter of the first window shutter to loosen it. Eventually it fell out and he caught it with both wings.

At that moment out of the corner of his eye he spied the Elder, Seth. The Gurglewobbler was asleep in his bed in the middle of the room, with an oval lump on the chest of drawers on the far side of this dark room covered with a dark blue satin cloth. Chad then lowered the shutter to the ground. Glad of a soft landing, he felt the damp grass between his toes and unloaded this heavy baggage by placing it upon the grey stone doorstep at the base of the Elders purple door.

Chad looked straight up at Boyce who was still patiently waiting on the branch.

"Okay. Ready Boyce," called Chad in a whisper. Boyce flipped his eye patch upward to get a better look on the subject.

"Ready Chad, here goes. Do or die!" Boyce shouted.

Boyce then proceeded to fly forwards on to the outer windowsill and peer inside. As he flew forwards into Seth's bedroom he failed to spot the said target in the corner, and within less than a second had returned to the outside sill.

"Have you got it Boyce?" asked Chad.

"Not yet Chad," Boyce replied, looking down towards the ground where his buddy was waiting, "Give me a chance. It's dark in there. I can't see it."

"For goodness sake Boyce, get a grip. It's under the blue satin cloth on the chest of drawers in the corner," retorted Chad sharply, giving Boyce the evil eye.

Boyce turned his head and looked straight behind him, "OKAY! I've seen it, here goes."

The room had been hollowed out of the tree trunk to create a comfortable, clean and tidy home. At the foot of the Elders bed on the wooden planked floor was a pair of dusty old black boots, waiting to be polished in the morning. Next to the chest of drawers was Seth's wooden rocking chair that had been a gift from his father. On the seat Seth had placed his silky smooth soft padded dark red velvet cushion, that was just wide enough to take his haunches.

Boyce approached the covered lump in the corner of the room and peeled back the blue satin cloth. He had kept his eye patch upwards to get a better look while he stood and stared at the jewelled egg. It was overwhelming. Boyce had never seen anything quite like this.

The turquoise enamel and the oval shaped red ruby gemstones with the crisscross bands of gold were awesome. "WOW!" he said to himself as his mind started to wander off at a tangent of thoughts of happier bygone days, when the rest of his family were still alive. What would they think of him now? Would they feel ashamed of him? Or would they be proud? The latter, I'm sure!

Suddenly coming back to reality and remembering what his mission was, Boyce produced his handkershute. He proceeded to wrap the precious cargo in it, using the string to tie and harness the package to his back, leaving wings and tail free for flight.

Seth was in a very deep sleep, and never heard a sound. He was dreaming of happy days playing games such as boules on the warm sandy beach by Wobble Cove with Livia, Leo and Talia. Hugo and Guy would be tinkering with their motor launch, *Moana*. Then they would all sit together and enjoy their favourite al-fresco meal of egg sandwiches, apples, bananas and cold cooked minted potatoes, washed down with a glass of Talia's fruit punch.

"Right, I hope I can fly out of here," Boyce said quietly to himself, checking everything was secured and pulled his eye patch back down and prepared himself to launch for a quick getaway.

Both Chad and Buzz were wondering what was taking Boyce so long. All they could do was be patient, and they didn't do that particularly well.

"Come on, come on, hurry up!" mumbled Buzz to himself, while chasing tiny tasty edible creepy crawlies up and down the branch outside.

"Ooh fresh meat, there is nothing quite like it!" Buzz mumbled as he gobbled them up in a hurry. He was concerned that the florescent dawn was fast approaching, and that the occupants of these tree houses would soon be waking up.

Boyce flew toward the windowsill, "Gosh, this is heavier than I thought it would be," as he stepped over the wooden bar to the outside sill.

Boyce lost his balance, slipped off the sill and was left dangling from the ledge with his wing tips.

"The weight is pulling me down, HELP!" he tried to shout quietly.

Realizing Boyce's predicament, Chad flew up to where his pal was suspended from the sill and supported him at his tail end, pushing him with the precious cargo back up onto the ledge, using sheer brute force.

"Keep the noise down Boyce. We don't want to wake those birds, or anyone else up," Chad whispered.

"Phew, that was close," Boyce replied, regaining his composure. "Thanks Chad," he added, as he unknowingly dropped one of his feathers onto the Elder Seth's doorstep.

Buzz had been watching intensely from his lookout. Boyce flew upwards to rejoin Buzz who was still waiting on the branch for him, then sounded the all clear squawk to Chad. This was the signal for Chad to replace the window shutter.

Chad flew back up to the sill and wedged the wooden

shutter back in the hole from whence it came. "Phew! success!" Chad exclaimed, "Looks like we have got away with it, and thank goodness those birds on their perches are still fast asleep."

"It is time to go home," Chad muttered to himself whilst retrieving his twisted crowbar from the neatly trimmed damp grass, and flew back to rejoin Buzz and Boyce on the branch to prepare for their homeward journey.

The daystar was now coming up and the early morning mist was lifting, and it was time to scram. The thieving magpies agreed to take the same flight path back to the north.

Their scheduled flight, for the time being at any rate, seemed to be going according to plan. The warmth from the ultra violet rays of the sun on their backs was a welcome relief after the cool dampness of the night. But it was not long before Boyce began to struggle with this heavy cargo on his back.

"I'm hungry! Core blimey! This weight is far too much on an empty stomach. I know what a paraffin budgie feels like now, with excess baggage. Can we stop for something to eat?" Boyce bellowed to Chad and Buzz.

Boyce's mind was dreaming of a bowl of crocodile sausages drowning in blackberry juice, with a sprinkling of crushed hazelnuts on top to give it some extra crunch.

"Sure thing!" came the reply from Chad who had been looking forward to in flight snacks of insects or anything else that moved.

Buzz was distracted by the magnificent view and was not really listening to Chad and Boyce.

Chad was flying slightly ahead of Buzz and Boyce. The thieving magpies had to keep going until they found a clearing in which to land, especially with this precious cargo.

Chad spotted the Mystic River up ahead, with an open green space between the tall larch and sprackling trees by the river's edge. They could hear the sound of the water lapping against the riverbank and the leaves rustling in the trees. The noise of the dawn chorus of insects knocking their knees together, resembled drums beating like a rhythmical war dance, as the magpie's lips salivated in anticipation of a tasty snack.

The long slender vivid blue ragdonflies watched the insect eating predators approach and darted to and fro across the water, seeking a safe haven to escape to. They had to 'hover and hide' from the intruders hungry spiracles, relying on their fast reflex actions from their tiny transparent wings to keep them out of harm's way.

"This will do very nicely. Come on hurry up, we can land here," Chad bellowed as he landed on the ground, feeling the long moist dewy grass between his toes.

As Chad looked skywards in horror he could see that Buzz was not going to make it, he was not paying attention.

"BUZZ, LOOKOUT!" Chad screamed.

"OOOUCH!" screeched Buzz. It was too late.

Buzz had clipped his wing on a large branch on his approach to the landing strip and was spiralling downwards out of control, catching his leg on a lower branch, then, CRACK. It sounded just like the crispiest of crackers snapping in two.

Boyce was nearest to Buzz and flew directly towards him, desperately wanting to break his fall.

"Buzz, hold on!" screamed Boyce.

Boyce quickly untied one of the strings from around his waist, destabilizing the jewelled egg in the handkershute in the process. Boyce had swooped upwards to where Buzz was helplessly flapping round and round in circles in the breeze.

"Quick, grab hold of this!" shouted Boyce, throwing him a lifeline.

Boyce felt his baggage shift. Buzz grabbed the string with his uninjured wing. Boyce was now above him. The jewelled egg slipped upwards and was now in the handkershute above their heads. They were quickly plunging to the ground.

Boyce clung on to the strings of the handkershute above his head with both wings so he could not fly. If he let go he knew the precious cargo would be lost. Buzz was hanging on for dear life, now being out of action. He was hoping for a soft landing, wanting to use the long green grass with any luck, like a trampoline.

Boyce had got his legs in a twist. He was trying to keep control, untangle his legs, make sure Buzz was okay, and hang on to the cargo all at the same time.

"BUZZ, GET INTO THE CRASH POSITION!" Boyce yelled.

"HOW DO I DO THAT FROM HERE!" retorted Buzz, feeling desperate and angry.

"IMPROVISE!" Boyce shouted loudly in reply.

Too late, they hit the ground with a resounding *BUMP*. The crushed leaves and twigs pulverized under the weight, no impersonations today of a bouncing bomb for Buzz.

Luckily for Boyce he had landed without injury to himself, or his precious cargo.

Chad could not bear to watch, and had covered his eyes with his wings.

After the noise of the crash landing Chad peeped through his wings tips and promptly rushed over towards his buddy to assess the damage.

"Birdbrain, what's the matter with you, you should have looked where you were going."

"I told you, I forgot my night vision goggles," Buzz replied defensively.

Chad pushed his beak right up close to Buzz's face and shouted at him, "IT'S BROAD DAYLIGHT!"

The sound of the crash landing had silenced the ragdonflies over the water. They breathed a heavy sigh of relief with the knowledge that they had momentarily escaped becoming a tasty morsel for these hungry birds at breakfast time.

"I've hurt my leg and wing," Buzz wailed, looking for sympathy.

"Is Boyce alright, and is the cargo safe Chad?" Buzz asked with a nervous quiver in his voice.

Boyce was shaken up, but otherwise was intact. He had recovered the jewelled egg and composed himself.

"Your tail is bent Buzz!" said Boyce, "and you are in bad shape, your wing and leg look broken to me."

Buzz was feeling rather sorry for himself right now. He knew he was in a pitiful condition, and to crown it all he was hungry. It didn't look like he was going to get his in flight snacks now after all. He wondered how was he going to get back with his companions in this state, let alone with the egg? Buzz was musing that this run of bad luck must have something to do with the broken mirror on the wall back home in the cave; and if the precious cargo were abandoned in favour of Buzz, both Cedric and Ajani would make his life unbearable.

CHAPTER 3

THE MORNING AFTER

The azure blue and cadmium yellow sky reflected in Wobble Stream in the early morning sun like a mirror image. The shafts of sunlight shone through the canopy of leaves emphasizing all the imperfections of gnarled bark on each Gurglewobblers tree house trunk. Each tree's leaves, danced like a troupe and unmistakable silvery veins were a common sight as the moisture slowly evaporated.

Seth the Elder suddenly woke to find the blue satin cloth on his chest of drawers had been cast haphazardly aside. Immediately realizing that the precious jewelled egg had vanished, he quickly put on his unpolished old boots and his crumpled blue 'thinking cap,' and was running around his tree house in a panic.

"What! Stone the crows! Where's it gone? I don't believe it!" exclaimed Seth, as he searched his tree house from root to twig, inside and out. "The culprits of this shall be toast, too boot!" There was no time for a cup of honey and nettle tea this morning.

Seth considered his options. "Hugo and Guy, are the resident pranksters, they are always into mischief. Could they be the culprits? Surely not! Even they would not be this hardboiled," he mumbled to himself.

Seth hurried outside and knocked on Guy's red front

door first. There was no answer. Next he ran over to Hugo's tree house, first making sure that he and Guy weren't practicing their acrobatics from the long rope that dangled from the top of Hugo's tree trunk. He passed the broken flowerpot as he scrambled up the rough slanted wooden planks to his orange door, *rat-a-tat-tat*. He knocked hard with his fist, as he tried to hang on to the door handle for extra support.

As Hugo opened the top half of the stable door, he saw Seth sliding backwards to the ground, still just about upright, but arriving back at the broken flowerpot, and scaring one of Loons tiny resident insects half to death.

"Hello Seth," said Hugo, popping his head through the top half of the door, then the bottom half of the door creaked open as the top half closed. "Hello Seth," said Guy.

"What's all the noise about Seth?" enquired Guy.

"Have you seen the egg? It's gone!" asked Seth.

"No. Is it to be boiled for breakfast? Two and a half minutes for mine please," Guy remarked jokingly.

"Have you thought of looking in the chicken?" teased Hugo, laughing. Hugo saw the funny side of everything, and always looked on the bright side of life.

"Stop messing about. This is no laughing matter you two. We must wake everybody up immediately," Seth said.

"Oh good, this is just like an Easter egg hunt," Guy retorted.

"NOW!" said Seth, raising his voice with exasperation. "We need to ascertain what has happened?" he said, rolling his eyes upwards towards the sky, and shaking his head from side to side at Hugo and Guy's indifference.

Seth, Hugo and Guy approached Livia's yellow front

door next, tickling the throat of her red and blue parrot Austen, as they waited patiently on the doorstep.

Austen let out a huge squawk, "Pieces of eight, pieces of eight, your too late, pieces of eight."

Livia finally opened her front door and the sweet aroma of cabbage and beetroot soup wafted from within. Startled by the noise, she looked at them through her huge bright blue eyes.

"Livia, Livia, the jewelled egg is missing. Have you seen it?" asked Seth anxiously.

"No, not since yesterday, but I will gladly come and help you search for it."

"That will be great if you would. We need all hands on deck!" said Seth, as he turned and spoke to Austen, "I don't suppose you saw or heard anything?"

"You suppose correctly, besides I have selective hearing syndrome. And no, I was sound asleep. It is hard work sitting on this perch all day you know, trying to stop myself from becoming bored silly," Austen retorted, as he returned to chewing his nuts and grumbling under his breath. "What a ridiculous question!" he uttered.

Seth gave Austen a stern stare and they all sallied forth to Leo's tree house next.

Seth hammered on Leo's blue front door *rat-a-tat-tat*. It seemed to take a long time for Leo to answer it. Whilst they waited on his doorstep, Seth thought to himself that Leo is such a sensible chap and that he would know where the egg is. Finally Leo answered the front door. Before he could open his mouth to speak, Seth asked anxiously, "Leo, Leo, our jewelled egg is missing. Have you seen it, or did you hear anything during the night?"

"Erh! No, Seth. I have not seen it since yesterday." Although Leo was fully dressed he was still yawning and stretching his arms as he spoke. "This is too early in the morning for this kind of caper."

"Come on, we have to find it, or it will be the end of our lives as we know it," added Seth with a concerned inflexion in his voice.

"There is only one tree house left to search and that is Talia's," Seth declared.

The little green and yellow cuckoo doorbell, Pinks, had alerted Talia. As they had both heard the commotion, she had already opened her green stable door. As Seth and the others approached Talia was already standing on the doorstep with an egg sandwich in one hand, and twiddling with her corkscrew hair with the other.

"What's going on Seth?" she asked hesitantly, noticing that all the Gurglewobblers were at her doorstep.

"It's the jewelled egg Talia, it's gone missing. Have you seen it?" asked Seth, desperately hoping that she would say that she had.

"I'm afraid not," she answered, as she spoke to her cuckoo. "What about you Pink's, did you hear or see anything unusual last night?"

"Well, you know me. Once I've had my supper of fruit berries, I'm out for the count. So no, I never heard a sound," he answered, still picking at last night's leftovers.

"They must have been extremely quiet if nobody saw or heard a thing, but I will join the search party to help you find it," Talia remarked.

Hugo and Guy had realized the importance of what had been thrust upon them all, and were now at least making an effort not to be antagonistic towards Seth and their friends.

Seth's heart was heavy with concern. What would his

ancestors say if they knew that he had been this careless? He had been entrusted as the custodian of this precious jewel, and had failed his kinsmen in his duty.

"We need to make a strategic plan, and naturally need to extend our search further afield," Seth said, trying hard not to sound too panicky.

They searched around the forest and had found nothing but a magpie feather on Seth's front doorstep. They didn't take too much notice of it, not realizing that it was a vital clue to the perpetrators of the crime. After all, it was not unusual to find a feather in the forest; birds would lose them all the time.

As they arrived back at Seth's tree house, Guy bent over and picked up the magpie feather from the sandstone doorstep. Seth looked up to the windows, and realized the shutters had been forced open in the night. Then taking the magpie feather from Guy's hand, they put two and two together. As the dawning of the realization hit home, everybody fell silent.

Seth decided that it would be worthwhile to travel to the southwest region of the island to the Valley of the Gems, and ask for assistance with the search from the Orchids and Flower people, after all, it would affect them too. Only he had been to the valley before, none of the others had ever needed to go that far, so none of them really knew why Seth undertook the same pilgrimage every year.

"We are going on an adventure, and I want you all to get ready. You will need to pack your sleeping bags because we will probably be away for a few nights! I will explain on the way," Seth said, addressing his companions.

Seth went indoors and packed his little pot of honey that he had collected from his own bees, together with sachets of dried nettles. He picked up his small pewter kettle and a box of matches, as he wanted to make a brew of tea along the way, stuffing everything into his blue bag. Before they left, Seth made sure that his beloved bees were safely tucked up in the beehives so they couldn't follow their master, as they could be prone to doing so.

The Gurglewobblers did not question their Elder and each individual went back to their own tree house, and set about preparing for their journey.

Livia quickly grabbed her wooden flask and beakers then filled the flask to the brim with the cabbage and beetroot soup that she had made earlier. She squashed everything into her yellow rucksack, but before departing she made sure that Austen had enough nuts to keep him well fed in her absence.

Guy picked up a bunch of bananas from his table, and stuffed them his into his red bag with his screwed up sleeping bag.

As Talia was packing the egg sandwiches into her green bag, she was thinking of all the times she had spent daydreaming about what lay to the north of the Forest of Bark. Now here she was, this very minute going on a journey, she thought it was very uncanny. Talia grabbed her flask and filled it with fresh water from the stream, she would top it up somewhere along their route if need be. She filled up Pink's bowl with berries, so he couldn't complain of nothing to eat while she was away.

Leo would contribute home grown cold cooked minted flavoured potatoes to the feast, but there would be no tending to his vegetable or herb garden today.

Hugo only had room for coarse ropes as they were rather large and bulky, and added a useful assortment of tools including his penknife. He would be relying on handouts from his friends to sustain him.

There had been no time to polish shoes or eat a proper breakfast this morning, so the food provisions were essential for survival.

When everybody was ready, they set off on foot toward their motor launch *Moana*, anchored at Wobble Cove, in the estuary, just west of the beach.

* * *

Now that everybody had left the forest, Austen and Pink's were feeling somewhat at a loose end.

"Hey Pink's, what's your favourite song?" Austen asked, while cracking his nuts on the doorstep.

"Rock around the clock!" retorted Pink's, "What's yours?" he said, as he scoffed down his bitter fruit berries with gusto.

"Polly put the kettle on!" answered Austen.

"Has anybody ever told you that you look like a technicoloured parrot with your coat of many colours? We should be calling you Joseph," Pink's exclaimed immediately in quick retort.

"How very Austen-tacious. You would be more useful turned into a clock," replied Austen.

"Cheeky!" retorted Pink's.

"It sounds like a definite case of sour grapes to me, because I'm more colourful than you are!" replied Austen.

* * *

The Gurglewobblers had been walking along the grassy trail that ran alongside Wobble Stream for thirty minutes or so. Seth told everybody to sit down on the path, and he would explain the circumstances in which they had found themselves.

By now everybody was so hungry and thirsty, it was time to have a bite to eat and a beaker of hot honey and nettle tea.

Hugo and Guy gathered some kindling from the edge of the trail, using Seth's matches to light the tiny campfire.

Talia poured the fresh water into the little pewter kettle, and while they waited for it to boil, tucked into some of the homemade egg sandwiches and soup, saving the rest for later, then washed it down with a great cup of Seth's energizing tea.

Seth began to divulge secret information to his chums about the existence of the Orchids and Flower people, and where they resided.

"That is where Queen Kohana and the Orchids guard the Amrit crystal base to our jewelled egg, the power of which provides us with immortality," said Seth.

"Oh, so that is where you go every year, is it Seth?" exclaimed Hugo.

Talia took another bite out of her egg sandwich, "Why is that?" she asked, talking with her mouth full, at the same time twiddling with the curly half of her hair.

"You shouldn't talk with your mouthful," piped up Livia, "Grandma Gurgle always said it was one of the rudest things one can do."

"Sorry, I'll try to remember that," retorted Talia, blushing as she spoke. She didn't usually forget her manners.

"Back to the story everyone. I know it has been my secret, but now that the jewelled egg has been stolen, I shall have to tell you why I undertook this journey. Are you all sitting comfortably?" asked Seth.

"Yes," came the collective reply. Seth took another sip of his honey and nettle tea, "then I shall begin."

As Seth began explaining to his companions, they all sat and listened attentively. Even Hugo and Guy were sitting still and paying attention, which made for a pleasant change.

They all tucked in to Guy's bananas and Livia's homemade cabbage and beetroot soup, which when swallowed gave an instant tingling sensation from the nutrients coursing through their veins. Seth continued,

"As you probably remember, every year I would leave the Forest of Bark for three days, and make a solitary pilgrimage to the south west region of the island to the Valley of the Gems. This is where the Amrit crystal base is hidden deep inside the first of the two mines there. The jewelled egg and the base are deliberately kept in separate places, thus preventing the egg from becoming too potent. The crystal base relies upon the ultra violet rays from the sun for solar energy, and when the egg is placed upon it, the Cabbergé jewel becomes re-energized, just like a battery, therefore keeping the equilibrium of life exactly as it should be."

"What does equilibrium of life mean?" asked Guy.

"That is one of those big words like wheelbarrow," piped up Hugo laughing at his own joke.

"Shoosh!" retorted Seth, "it means the balance of life," Seth added, in answer to Guy's question.

"So what happens now that the egg is missing?" asked Leo nervously.

Seth was sipping his tea as he looked at Leo earnestly, and then spoke in a whisper.

"Now I need you all to listen closely my friends, but there is no need for you all to fret. We and our island will eventually start to slowly change, but not immediately. Because we are thousands of years old and still look young for our years and have abounding energy, our powers will eventually start to diminish as we begin to revert back to our true age. Therefore our surroundings too will eventually cease to exist in the same way that we have come to know and love. One must not forget that the egg generates a vital protective shield that makes our island invisible to the outside world."

"What does that mean exactly?" asked Livia, as she topped up her friends beakers with soup.

"We will all gradually become weaker and die of old age, the correct term for it is extinction," Seth replied.

Everybody stared at each other and gasped in horror.

Seth continued to explain, "Even if one of the gemstones is removed, the aging process shall begin, not only with us, but our island too, becoming slowly visible to the 'New World' outside, bringing with it, who knows what? We do have one advantage though, and that is the perpetrators of this crime are not aware of this secret knowledge.

In the past only Queen Kohana and myself have been the soul guardians of this ancient lore, but in light of this situation, all of you now know," Seth paused momentarily. "So time is of the essence, and waits for no man. A bird in the hand is worth two in the bush."

"Can you define that please, Seth?" asked Talia, still twiddling with her hair.

Seth answered, "Cherish what you have, and know when you have the upper hand."

There was a moment of stunned silence. They all knew in their hearts that they could not retrieve the Cabbergé egg on their own, and agreed with Seth that the only realistic option open to them, was to go to the Valley of the Gems and seek the help of the Orchids and Flower people. They had a very good idea who had stolen their jewelled egg. After all, they had found a magpie feather on Seth's doorstep.

Once they had all finished their al-fresco meal, they picked up their belongings and continued on to Wobble Cove.

The usual orchestra of sounds from the Loonatics and other creepy crawlies in the forest going about their daily survival just simply wasn't there today. The silence was deafeningly eerie. The leaves on the trees stood completely motionless, it was like the whole of the forest knew what had happened, and was holding its breath whilst waiting for some sort of reprieve or further development, one way or the other.

The Gurglewobblers were feeling much better having had something to eat, but their mood had changed from one of pioneering, to be replaced by a sense of trepidation amongst them all. They tried not to dwell on their predicament and focus on the task that lay before them. Getting to the launch was the first part of the first leg of their journey, then on to the Valley of the Gems.

Hugo and Guy decided to try and cheer up their chums by breaking the silence, and spent a lot of time on the way to the boat larking about.

They climbed trees and used their coarse hand-made ropes to swing from one tree to the next by making a lasso, on the pretence of practicing their agility skills. When they weren't in the trees they were sneaking up on Livia, Talia and Leo, startling them from behind and generally being a nuisance as they sung one of their favourite songs, "We are the champions, we are the champions."

Seth was walking slightly ahead of the group and trying to turn a blind eye to their playful antics, when Hugo sneaked up from behind and pinched Seth's 'thinking cap' off his head.

"Right! That's enough Hugo. You are always up to mischief," Seth said turning round and giving Hugo a long frowning stare, while at the same time placing his hands on his hips.

"I would like my hat back, NOW, please. You know I don't like to be without it!" Seth said crossly.

"What's up Seth, worried that you won't be able to think properly?" asked Hugo, grinning from ear to ear.

"Now, now, Hugo, you are not funny and there is no need for sarcasm, it is the lowest form of wit," retorted Seth huffily.

"Yes, but when one is speaking to the–," said Hugo.

Seth immediately cut short Hugo's sentence. "That's enough lip from you Hugo. We have to carry on." He then turned to speak to the remainder of his companions and asked, "Shall we continue on without Hugo and Guy?"

"Blimey, he's got some face," interjected Hugo, handing Seth's hat back to him and hoping to save his own skin at the same time.

"Thankyou," Seth replied, receiving it gracefully and putting it back on his head.

"Yes, more face than a totem pole," piped up Guy with a broad grin across his face.

Livia gave Hugo and Guy a sideways glance as she wagged her finger at both of them.

"Look, we all know how silly they can be sometimes. But we have to stick together, just like we always have in the past, and I'm sure they didn't mean it. It wouldn't be the same without them. So they have to come. And besides, we really do need them both," Livia said.

"We are sorry Seth," said Guy, "and we promise to behave from now on."

"Okay, apology accepted. Now let's carry on. We are

nearly at the boat," replied Seth.

The Gurglewobblers continued their journey down towards the cove. Hugo and Guy kept their promise and stopped larking about. The duo had pushed Seth too far when he was under extreme duress, and their own efforts to lightened the mood had not been appreciated. As they neared the edge of the forest by the mouth of the estuary, they came to a clearing where the trees thinned out. The trees were replaced by vividly coloured grasses all the way down to the yellow, pink and blue tinted sand dunes. They could smell the salty sea air and see the anchored boat from here, which had been left pulled up on to the sandy beach, tilting slightly to one side. The motor launch had been made by all of the Gurglewobblers some years ago from the dead straight trunks of fangel trees, ideal for boat building.

To avoid wet shoes and soggy trouser bottoms they removed their footwear, then rolled up their trouser legs before making their way down to their launch, *Moana*. They had to meander their way through the rock pools of water left by the sea on this corrugated landscape. How good it felt to feel the fresh salty breeze blow through their hair like a Mexican wave.

Livia and Talia were wondering where the giant clams were today, they usually littered the beach and there was no sign of them, which was most unusual. Hugo and Livia could not resist jumping in and out of the rock pools, and splashing their friends with sea water. The tiny fishes darted for cover, feeling like they were under attack, taking shelter where they could in any available nook or cranny.

The tide was almost exactly right for them to set sail. They threw their shoes in and loaded all of the equipment into the launch, then Talia, Livia and Leo climbed aboard. It was ideal weather conditions for a jaunt across the sea.

Seth, Hugo and Guy pushed the wooden motor launch out a little way before clambering in themselves, and set off across the calm sea with a strong refreshing breeze behind them.

Everybody settled themselves down on their wooden seats for the journey, which was going to take them around the southern peninsula into the Bay of Gems. Once they reached the bay at the mouth of the Orchid River they would anchor the launch on the seashore, and sally forth on foot in a northeasterly direction, to arrive at their destination in the Valley of the Gems sometime later that afternoon.

CHAPTER 4

BACK IN THE AOLIAN MOUNTAINS

High on Ajani Ridge the humidity and heat from the sun was exacerbating the stench from rotting carcasses. The time had come for Cedric to report to his leader. Cedric had spent the best part of the early morning pacing up and down, wondering where his thieving magpies had got too. "They should have been back by now," he mused.

Ajani was putting his talons up for a rest. His unimaginable angry dark cruel eyes were firmly fixed on his jewellery, all trophies of his evil antics. His mood was usually foul, and he wasn't any different today.

As Ajani sat soaking up the warm rays from the sun, he cast his eyes towards the ocean. He could see and hear the sounds of the waves crashing against the seashore, and was wondering what treasures would be washed up on to the beach today. It was the perfect day for his bandits to return with his prize.

"The higher the clouds, the better the weather!" said Ajani glancing in Cedric's direction from the corner of his large beady black eye.

"CEDRIC," shrieked Ajani, "HERE, NOW!" he bellowed.

Cedric nervously shuffled over towards his master. "Yes sir," he answered, desperately trying not to sound too petrified.

"WHERE'S MY JEWELLED EGG, CEDRIC?" Ajani barked, "AND WHERE ARE THOSE THIEVING SERVANTS OF MINE?" Ajani was extremely agitated, and tapping his talons on the ground with impatience.

"I'm sure they won't be too long. Can I get you anything while we are waiting sir?" Cedric asked nervously.

Ajani's glazed cruel eyes softened as he gazed admiringly at his talons adorned with gold rings and gemstones, distracting him momentarily. He saw his own reflection in the jagged cracked glass of the fob watch sited by the nest. "I'm such a handsome beast, trim, tall, and terrific!" he said, smugly smiling, and egotistically wobbling his head from side to side.

"Yes Cedric. Fetch me some meat, and make it snappy," Ajani said, coming back to reality.

"That will be crocodile entrails then, sir!" replied Cedric.

"Hmm!" Ajani grunted, smirking at the thought.

At this precise moment Jalen popped his head out from the cave entrance having woken from his nap. Observing that Ajani was in his usual mood he decided it would be prudent to stay as far away from him as possible for the moment. Chad had been showing him some new skills the day before, and he wanted to practice them.

"I know what I can do," Jalen said to himself. "To start with I shall practice my balancing skills on one leg, using my small red and blue wooden egg that Chad made me!"

He hopped over to his box of toys and lifted the lid becoming distracted by its contents, and emptied all the toys on to the grimy gritty floor.

"I had forgotten about this," Jalen said, picking up a

very large green sweatband. "Chad said I could use it as a catapult when I'm older, whatever that is?" he paused momentarily. "Oh look," he exclaimed, picking up two small tubes, "here are my red and blue poster paints. And look at this! My red handkerchief," Jalen said excitedly, shaking the dust off it.

Jalen at last found what he was looking for.

"Ah ha, here we are!" he said chirpily. He grabbed hold of his little blue and red zigzag patterned egg, placing it on the ground. The little egg immediately fell over. Jalen stood it upright again, replacing it in the same position as before, and low and behold it fell over again.

Jalen stood scratching his head for a moment.

"Why won't it stand upright?" he asked himself.

"I know, if I make a hole in the ground to the correct shape, the egg should stand up." He found a soft dirt spot near the entrance of the cave, and with the tip of his wing scooped a small circle to fit the base of the egg into.

"Here goes!" Jalen squealed, as he tried to jump on to the egg. Jalen was clinging on tightly with his wings and claws with his tail feathers pointing upwards. He immediately slipped off, falling forwards to the ground, banging his beak on impact as the egg rolled on top of him. Jalen quickly recovered himself, jumping back up on to his feet. He proceeded to make a deeper hole for the egg and tried again. This time he flapped his tiny wings up and down, and at the same time jumped on to the top of his egg. He wobbled all over the place, first on one talon then on the other, trying to keep control.

"OHHHHH, TIIIMBEEERRRRR!" he cried, as he slipped to the ground for the second time.

"This is harder than it looks," said Jalen.

Both Ajani and Cedric looked up at each other, then both looked towards the entrance of the cave.

"WHAT'S THAT RACKET ALL ABOUT?" screeched Ajani.

"Sounds like Jalen is practicing his balancing skills sir," Cedric replied apprehensively.

"My, my, that doesn't sound very successful then!" said Ajani, with an evil grimace, spitting his words out abruptly.

"I'll just go and see if he is alright," said Cedric, glad of the opportunity to get away from Ajani.

Cedric went to the mouth of the cave and found Jalen sitting on the ground with a stunned look on his face.

"What's happened Jalen?" asked Cedric, being slightly put out.

"I'm trying to balance on my wooden egg Uncle Cedric," he said.

"I'm not your Uncle. Here, let me show you, feather brains!" said Cedric tiresomely. Jalen pouted, not quite understanding Cedric's remark, then stood back and watched Cedric's performance, hoping to pick up a tip or two.

Cedric was ready to show off and took a running jump towards the target. But instead of landing on the top of the wooden egg, he tripped straight over it. His hat fell off as he landed beak first in the dirt. Cedric found himself in a very undignified pose. His tail feathers were pointing upwards and his wings were sprawled horizontally to the ground. Jalen roared with laughter.

"Good show Cedric!" said Jalen, still chuckling.

"Well, I suppose you think that's funny. You had better wait until Chad returns to show you how to do it properly then," Cedric retorted in a huff. Cedric was feeling embarrassed and picked up his hat from the ground, and sloped off outside.

"Well I have more important things to think about than you, right now Jalen," Cedric muttered as he left.

Jalen sat and pondered his difficulties for a while. "I am trying too hard. Let's try the gentle approach!"

Jalen persevered. On his final attempt at jumping on top of his little wooden egg, he wobbled unsteadily. He carefully lifted one claw, then the other in turn, outstretching his tiny wings to balance.

"Wow, look at me!" he shouted with delight, clapping his wings together to applaud himself. "WHOA, WHOA!" Jalen squealed, "I've done it. I've done it. Look at me! I'm the king of the castle. You're the dirty rascal!" he exclaimed.

Jalen became very excited over his personal triumph. As he jumped off the egg he lost his footing, losing his balance and stumbling on touchdown. He rolled over backwards on to his tail feathers, still laughing, and couldn't wait to tell Chad when he returned.

"He will be so proud of me. I'm feeling a bit tired now, so I think I'll sit and rest awhile." Jalen mused. In no time at all he was fast asleep.

CHAPTER 5

THE CRASH SITE

Boyce and Chad were still deciding what to do with Buzz.

"We can't leave him here like this. If we go back empty handed, we'll be chump change," said Boyce.

"I know, but what have we got with us that we can use to carry him back with?" asked Chad.

"We've only got the handkershute, the u-bend shaped crowbar and some string," retorted Boyce.

"We could put Buzz in the handkershute and rest the egg on top of him, then tie it to your undercarriage," Chad declared.

"I can't do that. It'll be too heavy, and besides I shall never get off the ground, excess baggage and all that, or what! I'll probably just end up chasing my tail!" exclaimed Boyce.

"Got any better ideas?" Chad asked.

"Not right this minute," replied Boyce.

"Hey, what are you talking about over there?" interrupted Buzz, looking at his pals.

"What to do with you!" cried Chad and Boyce together in unison, both standing there with their wings on their hips and scowling.

"Well you can't leave me here, I'll die." squawked Buzz.

"Don't tempt me!" said Chad quietly.

"That's enough Tom Foolery from you!" Boyce said, turning towards Buzz.

"My name is not Tom Foolery, whoever he is! This is another fine mess Cedric has got me into." But as Buzz lay there injured he felt too broken to argue.

"Got it!" said Chad decisively. "We will find some twigs and small branches to make a stretcher to lay Buzz on. With the surplus string from your handkershute we can tie it all together, then I can straighten my crowbar and use it as a splint for Buzz's broken leg. How's that for an idea?"

"It's a good theory," answered Boyce, "but what are we going to attach it to?"

"To my underside Boyce! At one end I shall have the string tied behind my wings, and at the other end, the string shall be attached around by bottom in front of my tail feathers," retorted Chad.

"Yuk! Chad's bottom, that could be dangerous!" Buzz thought. "PHEW!"

"Sounds like a plan. Let's get on with it then," said Boyce enthusiastically.

Both magpies set tirelessly to work.

Chad scouted around for the correct size twigs and branches, and trimmed them to size with his blade on his amulet. He then cut the surplus string from Boyce's handkershute. Between them they weaved everything together till the stretcher was completed and the splint in place. Chad tied Boyce's handkershute with the precious cargo in it to Boyce's back, leaving his wings unobstructed for flying. They slid Buzz on to the stretcher. Chad straddled his legs so that Buzz was between them, and then proceeded to tie the string accordingly to Chad's undercarriage.

"Ready Boyce?" asked Chad, "Ready Buzz?"

"Yes," they replied.

"Ok, this is it. Let's go," Chad said.

They took off homeward bound, having had no in flight snacks or liquid refreshments. As they flew in the direction of the Aolian Mountains, both Chad and Boyce were getting very tired. It was such hard work trying to keep airborne with this additional baggage, but they would soon be back on home territory. And to cap it all, Buzz was moaning. "I feel airsick flying in this position Chad," he uttered.

"Too bad, old boy, you will just have to lump it. This is the best I can do mate," Chad replied, choosing to ignore his buddy's pleas.

Cedric was nervously pacing up and down, looking upwards towards the sky when he saw Chad approaching first. Chad had barely set his claws down on terra firma when Cedric shouted, "WHAT IS THAT?" pointing at Buzz, "What happened? And where is Boyce with the cargo?"

"Give me a chance, one question at a time please!" answered Chad impatiently. "Buzz met with an accident, and Boyce will be here any minute with the booty."

At that precise moment Boyce was closing in to land on the ridge. He was gasping for breath from exhaustion while struggling with the weight from his cargo.

Buzz didn't look too good. Cedric helped Boyce untie the precious cargo first, as he would be the acting baggage handler of the day. Cedric ordered Boyce to take the precious cargo into the cave and get himself some liquid refreshment, and something to eat. Cedric then attempted to assist Chad in tending to Buzz.

Boyce was absolutely famished.

"Now for some tucker!" Boyce exclaimed, reaching

for a platter of crocodile sausages. He drizzled pure blackberry juice all over them, just like lashings of gravy all over one's roast beef dinner.

"Coo! These are nice!" he said, scoffing them back ten to the dozen, without taking a breath.

"Best leave some for Chad!" Boyce uttered out loud to himself, starting on his bowl of crushed nuts.

Cedric untied the stretcher from Chad's undercarriage, and between the two of them dragged Buzz inside the cave and left him there on the dirt floor.

Jalen, wanting to help, picked up his red handkerchief to use as a sling and brought mud in from outside to make a cast. "We can use my red paint to colour it," Jalen said enthusiastically, putting it down ready for Chad to use.

Ajani's ears pricked up at the commotion. He stood there flapping his wings with anticipation and shrieking with delight at this triumph.

Once Cedric, Chad and Boyce had made Buzz comfortable they went over to report to Ajani.

"Well. What took you so long?" barked Ajani, "and what happened to Buzz?"

"Oh, not a lot!" answered Chad. He did not want his leader to know that they had nearly bungled the operation. "Buzz will be fine in time sir," Chad added nonchalantly.

"We have got the prize," said Boyce excitedly, and belching loudly. Boyce jumped up and down, feeling extremely proud that they had pulled the mission off successfully.

"Let us bring it to you now," exclaimed Cedric.

They sloped off and brought the cargo from inside the cave, and placed it in Ajani's nest. Ajani's eyes lit up.

"It is more beautiful than I ever imagined, and THE

GOLD-OOH, THE GEMS! This is a good as it gets," Ajani shrieked, while rubbing the tips of his wings together with delight. He gently rolled it this way and that to appreciate the whole egg in it's full glory. Ajani and the magpies did not realize the true magnitude and awesome power that the egg possessed, or that the Amrit crystal base was required to en-power it.

"Now boys," Ajani said, "when the Gurglewobblers wake up this morning and realize their precious egg has been stolen, they will no doubt start a search to recover it, and we will be ready for them, won't we Cedric?" he said, pushing his face in Cedric's face, beak to beak, his big black ruby eyes rolling back and forth.

"And how will we be ready Cedric?" asked Ajani, with a sarcastic tone in his voice.

"I'm not sure yet, sir!" answered Cedric nervously, his knees crashing together like a pair of symbols.

"YOU ARE NOT SURE, hmm! Let me tell you THEN. We will make a fake egg to use as a decoy Cedric. Now get to work all of you," Ajani bellowed.

"Yes sir," they all answered together.

Chad, Boyce and Cedric scuttled straight back into the cave where Jalen was waiting for them.

"Thirsty work this, I could do with a drink," said Chad, as he headed straight for the barrel of Adams Ale at the back of the cave. "Ah, that's better," he said, guzzling it down. The cold refreshing water rushed down his gullet, like a rip tide flowing out of the estuary into the sea.

"I see you left me ONE sausage Boyce, incredibly generous of you old son, thanks pal!" said Chad sarcastically.

"You are welcome comrade. Never let it be said that I am not all heart," replied Boyce.

"Chad, we need to make a crutch or something for Buzz so that he can get about!" piped up Jalen.

"Yes, little fella, we do. I'll tell you what, you go and find a couple of small branches and we will make it together. Meanwhile Cedric, Boyce and I have to come up with materials to make a replica egg," answered Chad.

* * *

Jalen scurried off to see what he could find to make the crutch with, and soon came back fully equipped with two long thin sticks and a roll of twine to tie it all together.

Chad made a sling for Buzz, using the red handkerchief that Jalen had found in his toy box. Between the two of them, they then produced a mud cast to bind Buzz's broken leg together. As a final touch they would paint it red so that everything matched. Both Jalen and Chad had made Buzz comfortable in his hammock, then used Chad's blade from his amulet to cut the sticks to size. Between the two of them they tied the sticks together with twine. "There, that'll do it," Chad remarked to Jalen. "Now go and leave it next to Buzz's hammock," he said, "but there is nothing I can do about his tail feathers for the moment."

Jalen crept in very quietly and placed the crutch against the wall by the hammock where Chad had said. By now, Buzz was so exhausted from his ordeal that he was deep in the land of nod.

"That will make a nice surprise for him when he wakes up." said Jalen.

"Now back to this replica egg," Chad exclaimed.

"What are we gonna use?" asked Boyce.

The remaining servant warriors put their heads together and subsequently came up with an idea, and very industriously set to work for the second time today.

Chad being the strongest, scouted for a large chunky piece of tree trunk. He used his blade to carve the wood to the correct size and shape, then with the help of Jalen, successfully stuck the shiny coloured paper on with sticky tree sap.

"WOW, that's impressive," said Boyce.

The magpie servants were certain that their work of art was up to scratch. Chad carried the replica egg over to show Ajani the results, and with his approval swapped their egg for the real one. Unbeknown to Buzz, Chad placed the genuine article in the cave beneath his hammock.

The Valley of the Gems

CHAPTER 6

IN THE VALLEY OF THE GEMS

The dawn was breaking across the valley as the early birds were catching the worms. The orchids began slowly waking up in their warm tropical heartland that lay between two mountain ranges. The Valley of the Gems stretched right across from the Lowlands to the north of the valley, all the way down to the south eastern region of the island, curving round them like a crescent moon.

During the night there had been heavy dew on the lush green fertile pastures. The Orchid River that flowed through their lands reflected the cobalt blue from the sky. The sun was peeking through the veil of leaves on the treetops, creating a kaleidoscopic spectrum of colour on all that lay on the forest floor. The refracting light on the shimmering rock formations resembled sparkling gemstones, and brought with it the sweet fresh fragrances from all the flowers and foliage.

The epiphytic orchids use the trees like towering tenement blocks to sleep in, with the exception of General Joe, who is an elderly orchid and much preferred to sleep in his tent on the forest floor. It reminded him of bygone days when he was on active service in the field, practicing jungle warfare.

General Joe had woken from his slumber before the other inhabitants of the forest this morning. He had a feeling that today was going to be a special day, he didn't know why; it was just good old fashioned instinct.

The General slid out from his snug warm blue sleeping bag, and started preparing himself for the day ahead. He slipped into his red tunic that displayed his victorious medals, and fastened the brass buttons. He wore a magpie feather with great pride in his top pocket as a permanent memento of a previous successful campaign. The General's eyes are very large and hide behind a wrinkly face and drooping moustache. The monocle that dangled from his neck reached all the way down to his brass buckled belt round his waist, holding up his baggy blue pants, stopping just short of his hairy knobbly knees. He put on his long black shiny boots that covered his red and black holey striped socks that he slept in, and poked his face out of his tent. The General then sloped over to his kit bag and baton that were propped up against a nearby tree. He rummaged around in his bag for a small hairy soft leaf to dry his face with, and walked the few paces to the river's edge. He knelt down and scooped up handfuls of fresh invigorating water to splash all over his face.

"A good General always sprinkles his face with water, to keep himself as fresh as a daisy," he said.

While he was down at the riverbank between two boulders he noticed that Zena, a red-hot poker and one of the Flower people, was stirring from her slumber in the early morning sun. General Joe bid her good morning as he dried his face. She responded by outstretching her arms, yawning and then smiled at him.

"Good morning General, I do feel groggy this morning," said Zena, blinking her eyes at him.

"Why is that my dear?" asked the General, still drying his face.

General Joe

"I must have had too much of Kiandra's home- made herbal brew last night," answered Zena.

"Never mind my dear. What you need is a good old-fashioned helping of water. That will make you feel much better," General Joe retorted.

"You are probably right, you usually are," Zena replied, getting up.

Once properly awake, Zena is full of an unrivalled energy. She wears an orange pointed hat and a green flowing body suit made from green leaves. The orange ribbons that flow from her shoulders blow wildly around in the breeze.

On this beautiful sunny morning Kiandra, who is an orchid and protector of the forest with a thoughtful and dynamic enthusiasm for life, was taking her usual early morning perambulation on the trail around the periphery of the forest, in the direction of the beach. She was enjoying wearing the latest summer fashion of a yellow and red spotted bodice, choker and shoes that contrasted with her billowy green trousers. She would stop every now and again to pick plant leaves for her herbal tonics. Once the brew was complete and fed to the plants, it would keep the forest inhabitants in perfect health. She recalled how her mother had taught her to forage all those years ago, and she would say, "The worse it tastes, the better it is for you."

How Kiandra still missed her kind genteel ways. She was bending down on the edge of the trail collecting more succulent leaves to add to her bundle, and looked up to see six little figures fast approaching in the distance. As they got nearer she recognized Seth, but not his companions. Seth and his band of friends waved at her, and returning the wave Kiandra stood and waited for them to arrive.

"Hello Seth, what brings you here at this time of the year?" she enquired, looking quizzically at the small group of people standing before her.

"Hello Kiandra, let me introduce you to the rest of my friends, the Gurglewobblers," Seth replied.

Once the introductions were over Seth said, "We are on an urgent mission and we must speak to Queen Kohana at once. Please will you take us to her?"

"Of course Seth, come on all of you," answered Kiandra, and led them back through the forest to present them to her queen.

After a short walk they arrived at a clearing in the centre of the forest. Hugo remarked on the colours of the rocks, likening them to an artiste's palette, loaded with different colours and shades, and noticed how tall the trees were here.

"These are good for climbing," he whispered into Guy's ear, hoping that nobody else had heard him.

"Aren't they just," retorted Guy, whispering back to Hugo.

"I don't think we will be able to play knock down ginger here tonight Guy," Hugo exclaimed, somewhat disappointed.

"You're right there," Guy retorted promptly.

Seth had overheard Hugo and Guy.

"Don't even think about it you two!" said Seth. He knew only too well what they could be like, and had had enough of their shenanigans already.

Now that they had arrived at the destination, Kiandra asked them all to wait. She went to inform the Queen that Seth and his companions had arrived unannounced, and that Seth had requested an interview with her.

Queen Kohana appeared wearing her vibrant yellow and red spotted layered petal kimono, with a blue sash wrapped around her slim waist. The expression upon her face was one of concern as she approached to greet her guests.

Livia and Talia thought how beautiful she looked with her pale complexion and red pollen rouge cheeks, that contrasted against her jet-black hair tied up in a bun.

The sun was now at its zenith, and with this heat the forest had now taken on a familiar musty smell.

"Greetings Seth. What brings you to our forest at this time of the year?" Queen Kohana asked.

Seth introduced his companions to her, and then stepped to one side taking Queen Kohana's arm, and drew her away from the rest of the group.

"Can I speak with you alone, Your Majesty?" asked Seth.

"Yes, you may!" Queen Kohana replied, "Kiandra, take Seth's friends down to the river bank and make sure they are given something to eat and drink."

Kiandra instantly obeyed her Queen and led the remaining companions down to the water's edge where they were glad sit and rest a while. The Gurglewobblers put their bags and equipment down on the lush green grass, and made themselves comfortable. They sat on the small stone boulders by the stream absorbing the aromas of their surroundings in this new exciting environment.

Seth was busy explaining the predicament in which they had found themselves to the Queen, and that they needed the assistance of the Orchids and Flower people to retrieve the precious jewelled egg.

"I suspect it was the thieving magpies from the Aolian Mountains, and that wretch they call Ajani. We found one of their feathers lying prostrate on the doorstep of my tree house this morning, and my window shutter had been forced. I am concerned for the safety of the Amrit crystal base in the mine." Seth continued to explain, "I am also convinced that the perpetrators of this evil deed are completely ignorant of the special power that the jewelled egg possesses. But since the theft, I have had to tell my companions the whole story, especially as they will probably be risking life and limb to retrieve it, Your Majesty," said Seth.

Meanwhile, Artie was hiding behind a tall leafy fern, and had overheard the conversation between Seth and his queen.

"Oh no! What have I done? What should I do?" Artie mumbled quietly to himself. As the realization hit home his heart sank, but opted to keep quiet and do nothing, hoping the problem would go away by itself. Artie's line of thought was interrupted when he heard his mother call his name. It was time for his lunch of jumble bee nectar, a rich mixture of berry juice and honey, and he must now return to the stem.

Queen Kohana called for Rafe.

"For safety sake Rafe, go and check in the mine to see that the Amrit crystal base is still secured!" she asked.

Rafe immediately obeyed his Queen's orders, and dispatched himself accordingly. Rafe's skinny bowed legs had corkscrew tendrils wrapped around them, and carried his wiry green torso at speed towards the mine. He knew that something was very badly wrong, or Seth would not be here. Rafe sped onwards with great energy and enthusiasm, his large oval eyes wide with alarm. His yellow dorsal sepals and lateral spotted petals blew backwards in the breeze, making his orange and red lip quiver from the vibration of his feet pounding on the ground.

Rafe returned within minutes after having carried out a thorough check of the mine and the crystal base, and said, "Your Majesty, all is well. Is something wrong?"

"Yes Rafe, there is. I would like you to gather all the Orchids and Flower people together at the water's edge, we need to have a tete-a-tete."

Seth and the queen carried on talking out of earshot from everybody, so nobody knew what they were discussing.

Rafe once again dispatched himself, and found Kiandra, Elie and Luella mixing a magical potion together. The large round pot was gently simmering over the dakota camp fire. The leaves and petals that Kiandra had collected in the forest that morning had been tossed into the brew, she was happily passing on her herbal knowledge to them both.

Luella is another member of the orchid family. As she stood and mixed the herbal brew with Elie and Kiandra, she carelessly splashed some juice from the pot on to her very large outer pink petals. As a result she had had to shed them. They floated down to the ground in the gentle breeze, revealing her crimson body jumpsuit. Luella then proceeded to tie her long yellow corkscrew curly hair back from her face with red flower stems.

* * *

Elie is nervous of her own shadow and is a Flower of the forest. Dressed in dark green foliage and purple shoes, she was busy adding more leaves and petals to the brew. The large fanned purple petals that surrounded her ochre face were like a sculptured frame around a mirror.

Rafe had now gathered the whole group together down by the riverbank where the remaining Gurglewobblers were patiently waiting.

Roxy disentangled herself from the tree that she been

hugging throughout the night to join her friends, feeling excited and very happy. She is a beautiful fragrant climbing rose. She wears viridian green leaf trousers, dark pink bodice with matching slippers and a pink rose bud hat on her head. The thorns on her arms and neck are so sharp that they can become lethal weapons, anytime, anyplace, anywhere.

Darva, mother to Artie and Banjo, was grumbling about her new lilac shoes, "Last year's footwear was so much more comfortable. I suppose I shall have to wait till next season to replace them."

Banjo looked up at her, unconcerned and remained silent, and turned his gaze towards Artie.

Artie was looking distinctly awkward and guilty. "What should I do?" he said to himself, "Best to say nothing for the moment, I think." He cast his mind to more pleasant thoughts, "which bush, battle or barricade story would it be tonight, and would he beat Banjo in their ongoing drinking contest of who could gulp down their warm pollen juice the fastest?" It was a pleasant temporary diversion for his mind.

The General had always given Seth a warm welcome. The two of them had become very good friends over the years.

General Joe made himself comfortable on a small boulder. He sat quietly listening with the rest of the group and placed his monocle into his eye socket. He felt it made him look far more distinguished.

Seth continued to explain their dilemma to everyone.

"I believe that the vulture Ajani, with his henchbirds stole our jewelled egg. Her Majesty and I have been discussing a plan to make a replica egg to replace the real one," said Seth.

General Joe spoke softly, "Pardon me for interrupting

Seth. As you can see by the trophy displayed in my top pocket that I have had dealings with magpies before, so I know something about how they operate. I believe we need to engage the assistance of Gazali, the Orchid Sorcerer from the East. He has such good magic, and is very wise. He may just be able to help us. I think it is worth a try."

"That's a brilliant idea General," piped up Leo enthusiastically, not even knowing who Gazali was; but any idea was better than none.

"That is an excellent suggestion General," said Seth, "are we all agreed?"

"We are!" came the collective reply.

Seth carried on addressing all his companions.

"We will need to take a scouting party to the east and speak with this Orchid sorcerer, to see what he can do to help us. The remainder of you shall stay behind for the time being to prepare the replica egg. On our return we shall make the necessary preparations, and set off in the morning to retrieve what rightfully belongs to us," Seth said.

"Who is going with you?" asked Rafe.

Seth decided that General Joe, Hugo, Guy, Rafe, Roxy, and Zena were best suited to go with him to the Mystic Mountains in the East.

The scouting party gathered their belongings together, and were going to travel light. All they would need was some of Leo's cold cooked minted potatoes and water to drink, as they were planning to be back by nightfall. It had been such a long fraught day and it was not over yet.

Once they were ready, General Joe tucked his baton under his arm, and they set off on foot to walk across the Grassy Plains, before reaching their final destination of the Mystic Mountains beyond.

Gazali

CHAPTER 7

THE MYSTIC GAZALI

In a time long since passed, the great tectonic plates that had once collided between the Aolian Sea and Gurglewobbler Ocean, had risen up from the murky depths of the seabed. The forceful and powerful energy from this convergence, created the gigantic granite Mystic Mountains. The gorge that divided these enormous ranges in two, filled with rainwater from the mountains, and forged the great Mystic River. The river flowed from the forest on the edge of the Lowlands into the sea at Mystic Point. Over time the wind had blown dust, and brought with it many species of seeds. The seedpods fluttered like swirling rotor blades from the west of the island, depositing themselves into the deep crevices, forming an effective landscape. Vegetation had sprung up as far as the lush green Grassy Plains to the south of the region, creating a sweet aromatic fragrance like sugar candy.

* * *

Gazali had been busy doing nothing by the hollowed out tree stump that was home, which is situated between a Rock and a Hard Place. He had been patiently waiting for the pea-souper to clear. Gazali sat admiring his beautiful deep blue silk gown that covered his orange and red hairy scrawny body. His misshapen magic wooden wand with the poisoned leaf that grew half way up, lay in front of him on the ground.

Jupitor, Gazali's old shire-horse, had been drinking water from the Mystic River, and was making his way back to his poor excuse for a stable. Jupitor acknowledged his master with a grunt and shook his sandy coloured mane as he passed him by. He had a contrary attitude, was rather large around his girth, and was Gazali's only friend.

Jupitor's stable was a cold damp stone cavern that was created from a bygone age. Fossilized fish and other creatures from the deep decorated the dank walls that encompassed him. Jupitor's only view from his jagged stable door was of the lush Grassy Plains. From this threshold, suspended from two rusty nails either side of his gateway to freedom, hung his bag of oats.

Gazali sat thinking and fiddling with the soft blue petals of his robe. He stroked his long grey moustache that grew from the sides of his bent nose and recalled what his father used to say to him.

"Son, always look after your crystal ball, and it will always look after you."

The time had once again come round to repeat this ritual of cleansing his crystal ball from the stepping-stones in the medieval stream. He would be cleansing away all the bad demons from his soul, but as per normal with most of Gazali's rituals and tricks, they had a nasty habit of backfiring. Unbeknown to Gazali this process had replaced his good soul with evil, making him self-centred, treacherous and greedy, the exact reverse of what was meant to happen.

Gazali got up and strolled down to the riverbank, carrying his magnificent ball in his hands. He stood on a steppingstone and watched the cold water gently trickle passed him. He plunged the orb into the water, at the same time rubbing the spherical object with his hand. As he gazed into his crystal ball he saw his bushy eyebrows and dark piercing eyes on his ochre and red wrinkly face, reflecting back at him.

"Mm, the reflection had changed somewhat since the last time I performed this ritual!" Gazali said.

Having completed this task he carried the crystal ball back to his hollow tree stump, and sat cross-legged on the floor to admire his lands.

In the distance he observed a group of travellers coming towards him down the dusty trail. As they neared his tree stump, he could see it was General Joe with a small group of Gurglewobblers, Orchids, and Flower people that were fast approaching.

"Ah, let them come!" he mumbled to himself with a smirk across his face.

Gazali stood up to greet his visitors as they approached, and called out to them, "Who goes there, friend or foe?"

"Friend!" General Joe replied, and proceeded to introduce his friends.

Gazali put them at their ease.

"Please be seated and rest yourselves from your long journey," said Gazali.

Once seated, General Joe put his baton down on the ground. Their host offered them a drink of water from a dried petal beaker, sipping some himself from his wrinkly mouth, while gently dribbling the surplus water down his red stubbly chin.

"So, what ails thee, and why are you so far from home?" asked Gazali.

"We are in need of assistance, Gazali," piped up Hugo.

"Quiet please Hugo!" said Seth gently.

Seth and General Joe between them explained the position that they had found themselves in. Gazali let them speak uninterrupted, not letting on that he had already seen their travesty in his crystal ball.

"Will you help us retrieve our jewelled egg Gazali?" asked General Joe.

Gazali addressed all of his guests collectively.

"The only thing I can advise you to do gentlemen and ladies, is to travel to the Aolian Mountains and confront Ajani and his henchbirds, and ultimately reclaim your lost treasure," Gazali replied, while gazing back into his crystal ball.

"What do you see for our future?" asked Rafe.

"Oh dear, the image has disappeared!" the now cunning and devious Gazali exclaimed flippantly. He turned his head away from the crystal ball and stared directly at his guests adding, "I cannot tell you any more than I already have, there is nothing left for me to do but to wish you a safe journey and a successful outcome."

The visiting party all looked at each other in astonishment. It was quite clear that Gazali was terminating their interview.

The General picked up his baton. They all stood up, thanked their host and left, to begin their return journey back to the Valley of the Gems.

In the back of their minds they had not been totally convinced of Gazali's loyalty to his fellow kinsmen, but there was nothing else they felt they could have done at this point.

After his guests had left to go back to their valley, Gazali thought that he would rather like to own this precious jewelled egg himself. He had seen all in his crystal ball, but was keeping it to himself. "That is my advantage," he mused.

"It is time for divine intervention!" he exclaimed out loud, knowing that there was nobody else around to overhear him, apart from Jupitor.

He picked up his red tattered leather bound book of spells that lay before him, mixing a secret concoction of ingredients together, then held his wand in his right hand.

"Time for some conjuring!" Gazali exclaimed.

Having overheard his master, Jupitor reached for the cotton wool and bunged it in his ears to protect his eardrums, exclaiming, "Oh cripes, here we go again!"

Gazali pointed his wooden wand at the mixture that he had placed in his large pot and began chanting.

"A flash in the pan,
Bang, bang, bang,
Explode with might,
See the sky at night,
With stars so bright,
I see a twinkling light."

There was a plume of smoke and a loud crashing sound.

"Oooh, this is not quite what I had in mind!" Gazali said, stroking his stubbly chin. A lantern appeared out of nowhere. Gazali held it up in his hand to admire his creation. "I can use it to light the way! But I suppose I had better try again. After all, practice makes perfect."

He raised his wand again to recite a different verse that he had adapted from his spell book.

"Let this stone on the ground,
Spin round and round,
May it land in a pool,
And conjure an imitation jewel."

There was a thundering roar that shook the ground and a tremendous flash of light.

"Ah, that's more like it!" Gazali said excitedly. The smoke cleared and a beautiful replica jewelled egg appeared before him.

"That's perfect. I can use this. I could not ask for anything better," he uttered, with a smile.

It was now time to prepare for the trials and tribulations that lay before him on his journey.

CHAPTER 8

THE PREPARATIONS BEGIN

General Joe returned to the Valley of the Gems with the scouting party. He was delighted to find that all the inhabitants of the forest had been very busy. In their absence their band of friends had created the perfect replica egg to replace the original.

With all this excitement nobody had noticed that Artie had quietly sloped off for a walk. He was following the same trail into the forest that he had taken a few days earlier, when he had come across the magpie Cedric. Artie was still feeling terribly guilty about his secret, and thought that he would be in more trouble than ever if he spoke up now. He carried on with his stroll to try and take his mind off the dilemma in which he found himself. Artie came across the little red and green shickleback that he had met before, and stopped to pass the time of day with him. He bent down to stroke his crusty whorled shell that engulfed his tiny body like a turban.

"Hello, little creature, do you remember me? We met the other day when I was talking to the magpie, Cedric," asked Artie.

"Yes, I remember you. You're Artie. I thought that you were going to eat me!" the tiny shickleback exclaimed nervously. "You frightened the life out of me."

"Oh, I'm sorry, it won't happen again. Anyway, I don't eat meat, so you are safe," said Artie. "Do you have a name?" he asked.

"No, not really, I am known as the shy shickleback, and I have never been given a name," the shy creature answered.

"Would you like to have one?" asked Artie.

"Oh, yes please," the shickleback replied.

"You are very small. I like the name Ickle? That sounds nice," said Artie, "and it suits you!"

"I suppose it does! Yes, I like the sound of that," he said, smiling proudly, "Ickle it is."

"I must leave you now, and be on my way. Good-bye," Artie said, leaving Ickle to his own devices.

Artie continued to walk by himself along the trail, enjoying his solitude. He heard a rumbling noise in the distance and stood very still; it was a sound that he did not recognize. Stepping behind a small boulder just off the trail he crouched down holding his breath in anticipation, waiting to see what it was. As the sound got nearer he saw a rather large brown shire horse with a sandy coloured mane, fast approaching. The horse was huge in size compared to Artie, and was pulling a two-wheeled wagon. On the seat of the cart sat an orchid in a blue robe, and he was singing a song.

"Oh what a wonderful morning,
Oh what a wonderful day,
I've got a sure fired feeling,
A little Cabbergé is coming my way."

"That must be Gazali. Where is he going, and what's that on the back of his cart?" Artie asked himself. Artie was now worried and kept very quiet until they had passed him by.

Artie decided that he had better head for home.

"Was it now time to be telling the truth?" but the thought of that idea made him feel rather nervous in his stomach. As Artie approached home he saw Banjo running towards him in a distressed state.

"You are for it now! Mum is after you. She has been looking for you everywhere. Where have you been?" asked Banjo exasperated, while pointing his hairy finger at his brother.

Artie sat down on a small grey sandstone boulder on the edge of the dusty trail with his head slumped forwards, cupping his face in his hands.

"Oh Banjo, I have been such a bad orchid!" he replied, hanging his head in shame.

"Why, what have you done?" retorted Banjo, looking concerned, then sat down next to him.

"Well, mm!" answered Artie nervously, "I'm sworn to keep the secret."

Banjo noticed that Artie was looking extremely awkward now.

"What secret? What are you talking about? I'm your twin brother, you must tell me," Banjo asked.

Artie raised his head and looked at Banjo with doleful eyes.

"Okay, Okay! A few days ago I was walking on the edge of the forest, when a magpie named Cedric stopped to talk to me. Cedric said he was a collector of shiny objects. Then he asked me if I had anything shiny with me. I said that I didn't, but then I foolishly told him about a precious jewelled egg that was kept hidden in the Forest of Bark. Now I have just seen what I think is Gazali passing by on a horse and cart, with something hidden under a blanket on the back, and the Gurglewobblers egg is now also missing. I don't understand what is going on Banjo? Help me, please, please!" begged Artie, with a whine in his tone.

Banjo stood up and took Artie's hand, "mm!" Banjo mused, "I'm not too sure myself. There is only one thing for it Artie. We must go home and tell mother all about it. She'll know what to do," answered Banjo, "We must! Come on!"

Artie got up and they both hurried home to find their mother.

A little while later Darva heard her twins calling her.

"What is it? Slow down," Darva cried, running towards them, arms outstretched to greet them.

"Artie has something to tell you mum," said Banjo, panting and out of breath, while looking his mother straight in the eye.

"No I have not," said Artie sheepishly, looking in the opposite direction.

"ARTIE!" said Banjo abruptly and feeling somewhat astonished by his brothers behaviour.

"Oh, you two are always up to something. Now which one of you is going to tell me what's going on?" asked their mother, giving them a stern stare.

Artie and Banjo looked at each other and frowned, then pointed their short hairy arms accusingly, and said, "HIM," both at the same time.

"Now that's enough, you two. No more nonsense from either of you! You will both stay here on the stem. Enough said, and that is that," Darva replied. Artie and Banjo gave each other a sideways glance and were silent.

This had now become *their* secret, and nobody, especially their mother was any the wiser.

CHAPTER 9

GAZALI IS ON HIS WAY

Gazali was happily singing along to himself. He began making his way along the track that runs alongside the far reaches of the Mystic River. There was a waft of acrid sulphur on the breeze that was drifting over from the live volcano in No Man's Land.

Jupitor and Gazali turned north in the direction of the Fresh Water Lagoon. As Gazali got further from his own territory the terrain became less undulating, with the variegated undergrowth that lay between the dense tropical trees of the forest. The warmth from the rays of the sun between the tall leafy trees on his back was comforting, not a rain cloud in sight.

"The perfect day!" Gazali remarked to Jupitor as they casually took in their surroundings.

The sorcerer's mind was focusing on rather more important thoughts. He had packed his spell book and the secret potion to perform his magic, together with his crystal ball and replica egg. There was plenty of nourishment for them both, and in Gazali's mind it was all they would need.

His faithful old shire horse Jupitor was pulling him and his cart along. "Such a heavy load!" Jupitor grumbled. Gazali, realizing that nightfall would soon be upon them said, "It is time to find a suitable spot to camp down for the night, my old friend."

As Jupitor sauntered on slowly, enjoying this change of scene, his ears pricked up and he spoke with relief in his voice. "About time too, I'm hungry and tired," he grumbled.

They had reached a suitable area on the northwest bank of Fresh Water Lagoon, perfect for both of their needs. There was fresh water for Jupitor to drink, and a good place to make camp for a decent nights rest.

The air had lost the acrid odourous smell that had drifted over them earlier, and had been replaced with a potpourri of sweet-scented perfume from the surrounding vegetation.

As the burning rays from the eye of heaven died away and the warm atmosphere cooled down, Jupitor finally came to a standstill. As Gazali stepped down from the seat on his cart, he tripped over the hem of his long blue silk robe.

"Oops! I would forget my head if it were not screwed on," he grumbled, recovering from stumbling and hoisted up his skirts to step forwards.

He struck a match on the boulder that lay next to the cart and lit his little lantern. He tethered Jupitor to a tree and fed him his oats, then fetched him a bucket of water to drink. Gazali then proceeded to settle down on the ground to read his spell book, and get a comfortable night's sleep under the stars.

"Now before I drift off to sleep for the night, I suppose I had better have a practice, so I can be sure of perfecting the magic for tomorrow's performance."

He opened his spell book and started to read it, then placed the magical infusion into his pot as per instructions written before him. He cleared his throat, tapped his wand twice on the rim of the bowl and began chanting.

"Fork of light
Knives of blunder
Give me smoke
And give me thunder."

A huge cloud of black smoke rose up from the pot, creating a mini tornado towards the sky. As the smoke rescinded, a knife and fork fell to the ground.

"Well, well, well! Will you look at that? Not quite what I had in mind!" exclaimed Gazali. He picked them up from the dusty ground and began studying them. "But they will come in handy as I forgot to pack mine anyway," he mused for a moment. "I had better try again. Here goes!" he mumbled, pointing his wand toward the potion.

"Sherzam, shazee, shazoo,
Zam-zee-zoo, taboo,
Give me a blazing bolt from the blue."

A giant plume of smoke erupted from the pot with such volition it knocked Gazali off his feet. He fell sideways onto the dirt floor, as a metal bolt dropped out of the sky, landing on the ground.

"That could be useful to fix the cart!" he said, picking the bolt up and dusting down his smooth silky robe. He prepared to start all over again.

Gazali was feeling somewhat bemused. He began pacing up and down, scratching his head with a puzzled expression upon his face, wondering where on earth he had gone wrong.

"I have got to get this perfected by tomorrow, or I shall be an absolute laughingstock. Here goes!" he said, raising the wand in his hand again.

"Leg of lizard
And eye of shrew
Toast his butt
Like a bar-be-que."

'CRACKLE, BOOM, WOOSH,' Gazali found himself perched on a lit bar-be-que.

"YEEE-OOOW!" he screamed. Gazali leapt off the fire, trying to beat out the flames of his smoking derriere with his hand, whilst running towards Jupitor's bucket of water to sit in.

"Holy smokes, that one backfired!" he bellowed, as the sensation from the cold water soothed his burning haunches.

"Backside firing, more like it! Great! Now I have a water butt!" Jupitor piped up sarcastically.

Just as Gazali was cooling down his buttocks, a thought came into his mind.

"Saints alive, I do believe I've got it! I know what's missing. I need some earwax!" he said out loud, releasing his haunches from the bucket.

"Jupitor, Jupitor," Gazali cried, as he crept up behind him.

"Yes master!" came a fearful reply from Jupitor, who wasn't sure if his nerves could take much more.

"Ah Jupitor my dear trusty steed. I need a favour from you. I just want to borrow some earwax."

Jupitor stood very still and rolled his eyes toward the stars. His hindquarters were shuddering at the thought. "What do you mean, borrow?" he asked.

"Well, I don't exactly mean borrow, I mean have.

After all, you are not exactly likely to get it back are you?" answered Gazali, becoming excited at the prospect.

Jupitor was now in such a huff. He had had enough. "If you are going to take some of my earwax, take it from my left ear."

"Very obliging of you my dear friend, very obliging," Gazali said, producing a spatula from his pocket and scraping out the required amount for his spell from Jupitor's ear.

"OUCH! BE CAREFUL! THAT HURTS!" bellowed Jupitor. "Oh the indignation!" he moaned, as his bottom puckered with the pain. "Give it up!" he said, shaking his mane from side to side, "can't you use something else instead?" he asked.

Trying to ignore his master when he was in this mood was impossible.

"Hmm, no, not really," answered Gazali.

Jupitor was relieved when his master had left him alone at last. "He constantly gives me such an ear- ache!" he said, as he settled down and carried on munching his oats, trying to relax a little.

"It's do or die Jupitor! " uttered Gazali strolling back over to his pot of potions.

"Hopefully the latter!" retorted Jupitor quietly, still chewing a mouthful of food.

Gazali had not heard Jupitor's comment. He was in too much of a hurry to get cracking on his spells.

The sorcerer rushed around gathering all of his secret ingredients together again, and added some of the earwax to the potion, saving the rest for the next day.

"Here goes!" he said enthusiastically, rubbing his hands together.

"Ooh, I've lost the page now!" Gazali declared.

Gazali flicked the scruffy pages of the tattered spell book over until he found the correct one.

"Right, this is it! Time to begin chanting," he said,

grasping his wand and pointing it towards the pot.

"Electrifying bolt of lightening
Very true and very frightening
Rain down on the nest
With eye of owl
Tongue of frog
Is so uncool
Come first light, I will have the jewel."

There was an ear splitting 'CRACKLE,' as the lightening bounced back into his pot. Gazali fell backwards on to his singed buttocks, with his legs in the air.

The smoke screen drifted upwards from his little pot like a ghostly serpent, with long smoky limbs that engulfed his whole body.

Jupitor reared up with fright, neighing rather loudly. "Core, blimey! What's he done now? making me jump out of my skin like that!" he muttered under his breath. Jupitor was having an out of body experience, momentarily looking down at his own skeleton.

Gazali had composed himself and got back on to his feet.

"Jupitor, it looks like the spell works, I just need to make it stronger next time, I need more bang for my buck," he said, clapping his hands together applauding his triumph.

"I know. I heard it!" retorted Jupitor sarcastically.

"We can now get some sleep, big day tomorrow Jupitor, big day," he said with enthusiasm, rubbing the palms of his hands together.

Gazali had to go over and settle Jupitor down again for the night. As he walked the few steps back to his little camp and tidied up for the night, he was thinking,

"What an adventure they had both had on this day. Who would have thought that the day was going to end like this!" and laid down in the cool long grass.

Just as he was drifting off to sleep watching the night sky, a shooting star shot right across the cosmos.

"That's a good sign, it's meant to be lucky. I shall make a wish tonight, and hope that it comes true." And soon he was fast asleep.

CHAPTER 10

JOURNEYING NORTH

"No time for polishing boots this morning Seth! Is everybody up and raring to go?" asked General Joe, as he packed the replica egg into his canvas rucksack, and put it over his shoulder.

All the equipment had been assembled the night before for a quick getaway this morning. The warm sun was coming up, casting strong light and dark shadows over the forest floor.

The search party had gathered together by the Orchid River and they were ready to leave. The Gurglewobblers had spent a restful night under the stars, studying the galaxy from the comfort of their sleeping bags. Kiandra had made them some pillows from soft furry leaves, to make them feel like they were at home. They had breakfasted on some of Seth's honey and nettle tea, with the remainder of Leo's cold cooked minted potatoes. The Orchids had had a good dose of Kiandra's herbal health brew, to fortify them for the adventure that lay before them.

Talia had secretly wanted to go with her friends on this journey. Although she had in reality, physically and literally come north, she really wanted to travel to the far end of the island, but General Joe and Seth felt that she would be more useful staying behind in the Valley of the Gems. After all, not everybody could go, and just maybe she would get her chance when all this was over. Instead, Talia set about showing Darva how to make egg sandwiches, and between the two of them they produced a pile for the rescue party to take with them. Guy had grabbed a hand of bananas to take as a quick fix snack, if anyone got hungry in their chosen mode of transport.

The rescue party said their fond farewells to their companions that were staying behind to protect the forest. Livia rushed over and blew all her friends a 'good luck' kiss, which was greatly appreciated by all. There was a sensational feeling of confidence amongst the rescue party this morning, mixed with a sense of anticipation.

It was not very far to the hot air Loon balloon, which they had filled with helium the previous evening in preparation for this morning's quick getaway, making sure they packed spare helium, just in case.

The Loon balloon stood out amongst the tall leafy trees, so big, round and red like a glistening giant garnet, as the brilliant sun refracted off it. The wicker basket was now packed full to the rafters with food and equipment, leaving just about enough room for all the passengers to squeeze in.

Once everybody was aboard, General Joe propped up his baton in the corner of the basket and placed the rucksack on the floor, securing it between his legs. He checked his compass to find north and licked his finger for wind speed. Hugo cast off, up and away they went, higher than a kite, shouting and waving good-bye to their friends left standing on the ground, and heading northwards towards the Aolian Mountains.

"Wow, look at that view!" said Hugo, pointing to the sprackling trees below them, that had bristling needles as stiff as bottlebrushes.

Guy was looking up towards the clouds high in the heavens. They reminded him of balls of cotton wool floating across the sky. "I have never been this high in my life before," he said excitedly.

"Anybody for a banana?" asked Guy enthusiastically, as he handed a piece to everybody. "I want the skins back though, could be useful in the future!" he said, gobbling one down.

General Joe glanced over to where Roxy was crouching down in the corner of the basket. "Are you alright my dear?" he enquired.

"I think so, but I am trying to keep my thorny arms inside the basket away from the balloon," Roxy answered.

"You'll be fine, just enjoy the flight," he said, helping her stand up, and trying to comfort her.

"I've never done anything like this before," she said, having composed herself. Roxy was clinging on tightly as she looked over the edge of the basket to admire the view.

"Neither have we!" said Seth, feeling the vertigo somewhat, and trying to reassure her.

Zena and Rafe were having the time of their life. They didn't know where to look first, left or right, up or down. They were soaring high above the treetops, noticing everything that was below them.

The fresh breeze that gently blew them northwards had an invigorating strong bouquet of honeysuckle. They could see the sea to the west of them and observe the flora and fauna below them. How exciting it was to be up here.

Guy and Hugo were still hungry after eating their bananas.

"Time to break out the egg sandwiches," said Hugo,

offering them round to everybody.

"I want the banana skins back first," said Guy, rounding them all up and stuffing them into his trouser pockets.

"These are nice," said Zena taking a bite, "here, try one Rafe," she said, shoving a sandwich unceremoniously into Rafe's bulging red lip.

"I don't normally eat egg sandwiches," answered Rafe, talking with his mouthful, not quite knowing what to do with it.

"Neither do I. Now remember to chew it. Don't swallow it whole, or you will choke. It will do you good, and besides, these are exceptional circumstances," Zena retorted kindly.

"Are we nearly there?" asked Roxy, turning to General Joe.

"Bit of a way to go yet, my dear," he answered.

Seth, having finished his sandwich addressed his companions in the basket.

"I need to explain the plan with you all before we get there, as we will need to enact it immediately upon our arrival." There was a pause for a moment then Seth continued, "Now listen very carefully. General Joe is in command when we land. He has had operational experience of ground forces, with much success. Over to you now, General."

General Joe, put his monocle back over his eye socket and cleared his throat of the remainder of his egg sandwich. "Oh! Thankyou Seth," he said.

"Now don't be shy General," said Seth encouragingly.

The avid listeners hung on to every word that General Joe said. Everybody had understood the specific roles in which they had to play.

"Any questions?" General Joe asked, looking at this courageous little group of friends.

"That appears to be straightforward then," added Seth.

Seth was secretly worried for the safety of this brave rescue party. "What if it all goes wrong? What if anyone gets hurt, or worse? I can't protect everyone all the time!" he thought.

As time passed, in the distance they could see the foothills to the Aolian Mountains. General Joe had spied what he had thought was Ajani's nest high on the rocky ridge above the foothills, and pulled out his telescope from his kit bag for a better look.

"There it is. What a fearsome looking place! Goodness gracious me, and it's so high up! We have a mighty task on our hands," the General said, stating the obvious. He put the telescope back into his kitbag, and placed his monocle back over his left eye.

Even though it was still early in the morning, the sky had turned a beautiful red colour with a huge yellowy orange sun, highlighting the smattering of clouds high in the stratosphere.

"Nearly time to land the balloon," Rafe declared, having just about managed to swallow his sandwich.

In a moment of excitement Roxy jumped up and flung her arms around Rafe's neck, almost cutting off his air supply. There was an almighty *BANG*, followed by a *HISS*.

"What was that?" shouted Guy looking around him, trying to work out where this strange noise was coming from.

Zena looked upwards to the balloon, and with a horrified expression upon her face, exclaimed, "WE'VE SPRUNG A LEAK! ROXY, YOU HAVE BURST OUR

BALLOON!" she said, glaring at her.

Roxy stood still, frozen to the basket floor.

"Oh no, what have I done?" she wailed. Roxy felt like the earth was going to swallow her up, and just maybe, it was going to.

The hot air Loon balloon immediately started to lose altitude. Everybody hung on tightly, as the basket blew in all directions out of control. The overhanging ropes were flapping wildly in the wind. The basket tilted to one side and Hugo fell out. He managed to grab hold of the rope, burning his hands as he slid down to the end, finding himself suspended in mid air.

"SAVE ME, SAVE ME!" Hugo bellowed.

"Where's the emergency exit?" cried Zena.

"It looks like Hugo has found it," Guy said grinning from ear to ear.

"The exits are at the sides, front and rear!" answered Rafe, indicating with difficulty, with his arms pointing in all directions. Roxy still had him gripped in a vice with his head tilted to one side.

Everybody was looking over the edge of the basket to where Hugo was dangling.

"HANG ON," they all cried together.

"Not much option, right this minute! This, looks like a guy rope to me," Hugo bellowed. He looked up to where his friends were in the basket, wishing he were still there with them.

Guy called out, "It's alright Hugo, it is only a tentative arrangement, ho, ho, ho!" laughing at his own joke.

Hugo's dangling feet were nearing the treetops. A branch twanged his bottom as he passed over it. "OUCH, OUCH!" he screeched. For a moment it looked like they were going to overshoot the beach and crash land into the sea.

Luckily for them they landed on the beach with a *BUMP*, just missing the water's edge. Hugo was the first to hit the sand. He was dragged, bottom first along the ground, skimming over the stones and broken seashells. He had his knees pulled right up close to his chest as he clung on for dear life.

"OW, OW!" Hugo yelped. It never actually occurred to him for one moment to let go.

The General's monocle fell out of his eye socket and was swinging wildly about like a pendulum, hitting him on his nose.

"Ouch!" General Joe yelped, grabbing hold of the end to halt the motion. He was clinging on to the edge of the basket with the other hand, whilst keeping his kit bag wedged between his knees.

Roxy was still embracing Rafe's neck, nearly strangling him to death, and Zena was cowering next to Guy.

Seth had grabbed the rucksack containing the replica egg, and was holding on to it like his life depended upon it, which was actually true, it did.

The rescue party were hoping and praying to land in one piece, and still be breathing on touchdown.

As the basket eventually came to a standstill, it tipped over onto its side in the sand, and the balloon lay deflated of air beside them.

"Phew! Soft landing then!" Seth said sarcastically.

They all bundled out to assess the damage, and promptly straightened out the wrinkles, till the balloon was completely flat.

"I believe this is fixable," said Seth turning to General Joe, "where is your repair kit?" he asked.

The General inevitably grabbed his kit bag from the basket, and was rummaging around searching for the pack of plasters.

The egg was safe, nobody apart from Hugo was hurt, and the contents of the basket were intact.

"What about me!" Hugo asked sardonically.

"You'll manage, pick yourself up and dust yourself off, you'll be fine," Guy said, unconcerned for the well being of his twin brother.

Hugo got up and soothed his rope burn with General Joe's magic potion, and joined in with his companions, and set to work to find the hole created by Roxy's thorny arms.

"Found it!" said Zena, picking up the damaged area of the balloon.

"I'm sorry, truly I am. I didn't mean to burst the balloon," Roxy wailed, almost in tears. "If only I hadn't got so excited!"

Roxy had caused enough damage already, and thought it best to let her friends carry out the repairs without her. After all they would not thank her if she snagged it again.

General Joe had finally found the plasters, took one out of his bag and stuck it over the hole. "There you go, that's that one sorted," he said.

The rescue party refilled the hot air balloon with the spare helium in preparation for the homeward journey. They made sure it was completely hidden from view, and decided it would be prudent to get off the beach promptly.

They gathered all their belongings together that had spilled out of the wicker basket on landing, and set off on foot to continue with their mission. In the back of their minds they were hoping that Ajani and his thieving magpies had not seen them entering their air space. The red sky appeared to be changing colour. The sun had disappeared to be replaced by strange looking dark clouds that were lingering over the mountain, which was unusual for the time of day. They were now off the beach with the Bay of Vultures to the west of them, and heading deep into the forest along the dusty trail, making good progress in a north easterly direction towards the Aolian foothills.

As the rescue party stopped for a rest in a small grassy clearing near the base of the mountain they heard the whiney of a horse, coupled with the rumble of cartwheels coming along the trail. They promptly removed themselves from the path and hid behind the spiky sprackling trees, quietly watching. As it drew nearer they saw an orchid wearing a blue gown sitting high on his seat, and he was humming a tune to himself.

"It's Gazali! What is he doing here?" asked Seth rhetorically.

Gazali had seen the hot air balloon descend from the sky in the distance, and thought that that was the end of the search party.

"This makes my task a lot easier," Gazali said, musing to himself.

"I wonder what he is up to?" asked Rafe.

Everybody kept very quiet and still, holding their breath until Gazali had passed.

"I don't think he knows we are here!" Zena stated.

"I bet he saw our hot air balloon descending from the sky, and probably thinks that we have come to a sticky end," Rafe piped up.

"I guess we now know which side he is on!" retorted the General.

"You are probably right Rafe, he does not know that we are here, which is to our advantage. So we need to continue with our quest, now," exclaimed Seth.

CHAPTER 11

ARTIE CONFESSES

Queen Kohana had been busy making sure that all her subjects were now in the process of fully protecting the forest from possible attack. She had placed guards at various strategic positions around the periphery. Elie and Darva played their part by keeping the troops well fed with egg sandwiches for the remaining Gurglewobblers, and liquid tonic for the Orchids and Flower people, washed down with plenty of fresh water. The traps had already been laid in the more difficult areas, but they had yet to construct the barricades, as per General Joe's instructions before he left, though nobody could think why. There may or may not be an attack from the north, it was a chance they could not afford to take, but the whole valley must be prepared, just in case.

The entrances to the two mines were now properly camouflaged, thanks to the valiant efforts of Kiandra, Leo, Luella and Talia. The four of them had been busy scooping up soil, using the thick sturdy leaves from the plant Tolip-in-Grandma's tongue, ideal for the task. They had gathered pebbles and branches from the forest floor to make a wild earthy concoction. The willow sticks were weaved together and tied with twine, then covered with the organic matter they had collected. It was all held together with the infamous mud mache, giving off a dank musty aroma when completed, ensuring the total security of the Amrit crystal base hidden inside. Once the task was finished they walked over to where the queen was sitting on the soft grass.

Leo approached the queen.

"You cannot see the entrance of the mines at all now, with the exception of a very small opening for our access, Your Majesty," he said.

"Good, well done all of you. Both mines must at all costs be kept a secret hiding place," said Queen Kohana, feeling satisfied that her subjects had done their level best to conceal the entrances.

Elie was nervously dithering around. "Can I do anything else to help Leo?" she asked him timidly.

"Most of the hard work is done now Elie, but we still have to be on the alert, just in case the forest is attacked from the north," Leo retorted.

"I don't fancy that idea. What do you mean?" asked Elie, twiddling her buds. Elie was in a panic, what could she do in such a situation, she thought to herself? Dithering around was what she did best. She was of such a nervous disposition, she could not even contemplate what she would do if their sanctuary were directly threatened.

"There is no need to over react Elie," said Leo, trying to calm her down, "We'll just have to take it in our stride. It may not even happen," replied Leo, offering her a beaker of left over honey and nettle nectar. As she drank this soothing concoction she felt her nerves settling down.

Darva had taken Banjo and Artie off their stems to hide them behind the heavily camouflaged entrance to the mine, for their own protection. They were so precious to her that no harm must ever come to her babes.

"Now I want you both to keep quiet, you'll be safe in

here, and you are not to move from this spot," she said with a no nonsense tone in her voice.

"Yes mum," they both answered together.

Darva left them in the cave and trusted them to behave themselves, as she carried on with her daily chores.

Banjo turned to face Artie. "This is all your fault," he said.

"How is it my fault?" retorted Artie.

"If you hadn't wandered off in to the forest and met *THAT* magpie Cedric, and told him of the jewelled egg, none of this would have happened," Banjo retorted with frustration.

"But Cedric promised me a reward," Artie replied, raising his voice.

"A reward of nothing but trouble and danger, after all he didn't exactly say what this reward would be, did he?" Banjo yelled back at Artie.

"Well, no," replied Artie disappointedly.

Whilst Artie sat thinking about his predicament, he was still feeling very guilty.

"It probably would have happened anyway," Artie said, trying to justify the betrayal of his kinsmen.

"No it wouldn't," replied Banjo, haughtily.

Unbeknown to Artie and Banjo, Livia and Talia had heard their raised voices. They had walked over to the mine entrance and were lingering outside, eavesdropping.

"Anyway, there is no use crying over the stolen egg now, it is too late. But what shall we do next?" asked Banjo.

A few moments later the entrance to the mine opened, and Livia and Talia stepped inside.

"YOU TWO!" shrieked Livia, "What have you done?

We both overheard what you said. You have endangered all of us, and you have jeopardized the safety of General Joe, Seth and the search party."

"You had better tell us everything that you know. I will go and fetch your mother and the others. Wait here with Livia," said Talia.

Talia sped off quickly to find Artie and Banjo's mother first. She told Darva what she and Livia had overheard.

"My goodness!" exclaimed Darva, aghast. "We must alert the queen." Her heart sank with disappointment, "I know Artie can be very defiant, but surely not Banjo."

Artie and Banjo nervously waited in the mine, their stomachs churning with fear.

"Wait till mother gets here, I wouldn't like to be in your shoes," Banjo said smugly.

As they heard the sound of footsteps fast approaching they sat upright, stiff rigid, their little hearts pounding as loud as a big base drum.

Darva entered the mine ahead of the others.

Before mother could say anything at all they both pointed their hairy fingers at each other, just like they always did when trying to shift the blame.

"It's him!" they both squealed together.

"I don't believe you two. How could you keep quiet about something this important, you have both let us all down badly," Darva said in exasperation.

"I was nothing to do with it, it was him," said Banjo defensibly, still pointing his hairy finger at Artie.

Poor Artie, he couldn't feel any worse than he already did.

"I know it is all my fault," Artie admitted, attempting to get Banjo off the hook.

Artie then went on to explain that although he had

told his brother of his meeting in the forest with Cedric the magpie, Banjo never knew until it was too late.

Darva interrupted Artie, "Cedric, so you are on first name terms with this bird, are you?" she said sarcastically.

Artie continued, "The magpie Cedric promised me a reward, but I didn't know it was going to turn out like this, honest, I didn't."

"A reward of what?" asked Darva.

"Well, he never actually said what it was to be." Artie replied sheepishly.

"This is a fine mess we are in. Here comes the Queen with the others," Darva declared.

Queen Kohana approached with a stern look upon her face. Artie had to tell her what he had done. She spoke softly but firmly to him, "You have betrayed us all Artie, the search party included. For the foreseeable future you both will stay in here out of sight and reflect upon your actions, till I can decide what to do with you."

Both Artie and Banjo realized that if there was a moment to keep quiet, this was it. They were not happy sitting in this cold dark mine. The only shaft of light that they had was beaming down through an opening in the roof onto the dirt floor at the far end of the mine, where the Amrit crystal base stood.

Elie had been chosen to keep an eye on these two mischievous rascals at Queen Kohana's request. The queen, understanding Elie's nervous disposition, explained to her that this task would be good for her. It was something she could do to assist her kinsmen that would not be putting herself in any danger. Elie sat on the rock outside the entrance to the mine, stiff rigid and did not move. She was quietly hoping that Artie and Banjo would not give her any bother. Her nerves could not stand it. Even the sound of the leaves rustling in the breeze was enough to make her jumpy.

Darva was feeling so disappointed in her sons, but eventually, at least, she could console herself with the fact that they had told the truth.

Queen Kohana walked back over to the grassy clearing by the river, and sat down with everybody on the soft lush green grass.

"It's all too late!" exclaimed Livia disappointedly.

"General Joe, Seth and their search party would have arrived by now. We have no way of letting them know what has happened," said Kiandra.

Luella spoke softly, trying to remain positive, "I think we should be more concerned with protecting our forest from possible attack now," she said.

"What do you think Leo and Talia?" asked Queen Kohana.

"The damage is already done now, Your Majesty!" Leo exclaimed.

"All we can do now is to think on our feet. We are as ready as we'll ever be," declared Talia.

The Queen quietly addressed these brave little individuals, as she did not want to be overheard.

"I cannot disagree with any of you, but we must be on our guard. The only advantage is that we are a considerable distance from the north. Even though our crystal base is safe, the perpetrators of the crime do not know that the precious jewelled egg has no power without it. The jewels are worth a fortune and must remain in place for reasons already explained. So we now must carry on with the homeland security," she said.

Two or so hours passed, and at last the forest was now finally secure. All they could do was watch and wait, living in hope that the search party would be successful with their charge. After all, their whole future depended upon it.

Chad

CHAPTER 12

JALEN'S TRAINING

Ajani was strutting around on the ridge with the full blast of the ultra violet rays beating down on his feathers, while admiring the jewelry that adorned his sharp talons.

The eggs had previously been swapped over, and the genuine egg was now beneath Buzz's hammock in the cave, hidden under a heap of hides. Inside the cave Buzz was laid up in his hammock, still having no idea what lay beneath him. He was deep in the land of nod, having his favourite dream of owning his own drinking establishment, serving Adams Ale on tap, with complementary snacks of berries, nuts, insects and worms to all the birds. Buzz had not told his chums of his dream. He knew that he would most probably be ridiculed. Besides it was *his* private dream, a place where only he could escape too. After all, every bird has dreams and aspirations, and now that he had permanently damaged tail feathers, could it now become a real possibility?

Cedric and Boyce were keeping a keen eye on the genuine egg from the cave entrance, while Chad was busy showing Jalen how to fly and glide on the thermals. Chad began by showing Jalen a few tricks on his skateboard. He was skating up and down the walls of the interior of the cave, from side to side and upside down, showing off.

Jalen stared at Chad in wonderment, and spoke excitedly, "AWESOME CHAD! Can you teach me how to do that?"

"You need to learn to fly properly first," Chad answered kindly.

"Teach me, teach me, pleeeease!" squealed Jalen.

"Ok! This is your first real flying lesson. Stand on my skateboard, flap your wings up and down and they will lift your body up," said Chad.

Jalen did exactly as Chad had instructed.

"I can fly, I can fly," declared Jalen happily.

Once Jalen was airborne he became so excited, he forgot to keep his wings flapping up and down. He immediately slumped to the ground. The sound of his BOOMPH! coup de grace left him stunned and with ruffled feathers.

"No, not like that silly, you've got to keep your wings moving up and down. Here, like this. Watch me," Chad said shaking his head from side to side.

Chad proceeded to show Jalen again how it was done. Jalen tried again and this time he got into the swing of it.

"Well done little fella! Now all you have got to do is learn to look tough and mean, just like a jewel thief," Chad said encouragingly.

Jalen tightened the muscles in his little body. He turned this way and that, puffing up his fluffy downy feathers and frowning.

"How's this, Chad. Do I look scary enough?" asked Jalen.

"Not bad, keep on practicing," Chad said kindly.

Chad secretly had a soft spot for Jalen, though he never let on to his fellow magpies. He knew that Jalen did not have one nasty bone in his little body, and that he would never make a jewel thief for Ajani, he was just too kind hearted and honest.

CHAPTER 13

SHOW TIME

Gazali had been the first to arrive at the foothills of this damnable mountain, not realizing that General Joe and his rescue party had survived their crash landing. He could not help but notice the sour odour emanating from the top of the ridge; it was so uninviting, compared to the fragrant lush green grassy acreage at the base of the mountains where he resided. Gazali's nose began to twitch as the smell from the rancid air wafted through his nostrils.

"We're not stopping, so I suppose it doesn't really matter," Gazali said, whispering into Jupitor's ear.

He tethered Jupitor to a tree and told him to keep quiet, giving him a cube of sugar as a bribe. Gazali stuffed Jupitor's ears full of cotton wool to deaden the sound of the noise to come. After all, Jupitor had had enough last night with his out of body experience, and his mood had not improved since.

The sorcerer gathered up his belongings and set off on foot, round to the eastern side of the ridge carrying a large bag with him, and began climbing all the way to the top. As Gazali neared the apex of the ridge, he was thinking to himself that should he pull this off, it would be no more than he deserved. What he had failed to notice was, that General Joe with his chums were watching him from behind a large red and blue scrollop bush at the base of the ridge, till he was out of sight.

"I wonder what he is up to?" Guy said, speaking to the General.

"Hard to say at the moment!" replied General Joe, stroking his moustache.

"He's got rather a lot of baggage with him!" exclaimed Hugo.

"He is bound to be up to no good," piped up Rafe.

* * *

Earlier that morning, Ajani and his thieving henchbirds had seen the approach of a hot air balloon in the distance, and observed that it had crashed onto the beach. They had naturally assumed that the occupants were no longer a threat as nobody could survive that, or so they thought.

The magpie Cedric had seen Gazali carrying a lot of equipment with him, sneaking up the eastern side of the mountain, out of the corner of his eye.

"I knew this would happen! That five petal creature, he's got more petals than brains," Cedric exclaimed to Ajani.

Boyce piped up, "Can we have him for snacks, one of our five a day," then looked upwards to the sky, "mm, how strange, it's gone rather dark for the time of day!" he said, fiddling with his handkershute, unsuccessfully trying to fold it up into a tidy pile.

Ajani gave Cedric a long evil glare.

"Let him come, this could be our only chance to get rid of him. And Boyce, be quiet, you are giving me a headache," he said grumpily, returning to pick at the scraps of crocodile entrails.

Ajani lingered with Cedric and Boyce by his nest, and was just not paying attention to the bigger picture.

Buzz had decided to join them briefly, having struggled out of his hammock, still in a pathetically bad way, and unfit for duty.

Chad had an instinct to remove Jalen out of harm's way, as Gazali was about, hiding on the ridge somewhere, and led him back into the cave and told him to stay out of sight, just in case.

Buzz limped back to his hammock to catch up on even more shut-eye, still not realizing what lay hidden beneath him. Boyce followed them back inside shortly afterwards, leaving Cedric outside alone with Ajani.

Gazali had reached the summit as the accursed black clouds that everybody had seen earlier were gathering pace. He laid out his spell book on the ground, and placed his cauldron next to it.

"This could be my lucky day," Gazali stated, as he poured his double strength secret potion into the pot. He threw in Jupitor's earwax, then picked up his wand and began wailing.

"Summon bolts from afar
Oh La-De-Da
May his buns be toast,
And forever roast
Thunderbolts of lightening
Very, very frightening
Go, go, go, go, go!"

There was an earth shattering, CRASH, CRACKLE, BANG! The bolts of lightning rained down on Ajani's nest from the sky above. A gigantic serpent of thick black acrid smoke engulfed the whole ridge. Ajani was startled beyond recognition, and with his feathers distinctly ruffled, scarpered into the entrance of the cave to where his henchbirds were taking refuge. Cedric without any hesitation was running right behind him, hot on his heels. This momentous whirlwind created the ideal smoke screen, as the storm continued to rage from the black threatening sky above.

Gazali ran down to the nest as fast as his little legs could carry him, trying not to choke on the smoke. He quickly swapped the eggs over and bundled Ajani's egg into his own bag, then made a hasty retreat back down the mountain to where Jupitor was waiting for him. It was all over in seconds.

"Well, slap my butt and call me Sally! That was so easy Jupitor. Well, we certainly got enough bang for our buck today, didn't we, my old friend?" Gazali said, still coughing from the smoke. He was feeling smug about this triumph, as he unplugged Jupitor's ears of the cotton wool.

"GOOOOOD! It must have been my earwax that clinched it," replied Jupitor.

Jupitor was still irked by the situation that he found himself in, and continued to suck on his sugar cube.

Not wanting to damage the precious cargo, Gazali removed it from his bag, and placed it on the back of his wagon on a bed of soft petals, covering it over with a blanket. He hitched up his skirts and climbed back on to the seat of his cart.

"Come on, my trusty old steed. Go east Jupitor, we're going home," he said.

There was no hesitation whatsoever from Jupitor as he galloped off at great speed.

Everything had happened so fast. Ajani and the magpies stood by the entrance of their cave livid with rage, having missed the opportunity to finish this blue petal thief off, even though they knew the stolen egg was a replica. It was the brazen nerve of the creature.

The magpies and Ajani slowly reappeared from the entrance of the cave, still coughing and spluttering from the smoke. Jalen was following close behind. Cedric carried a stone tablet to write on, a pot of Jalen's red poster paint to use as ink, and a quill to write with.

As the thick black smoke slowly cleared, Boyce stated the obvious while scratching his head to remove the bugs.

"One fake egg for another," Boyce uttered, "well, who would have thought it?"

General Joe and the rescue party did not realize at this precise moment in time that Gazali had swapped the egg in the nest over, and had actually escaped with one.

Lying low out of sight the rescue party had heard one heck of a kerfuffle, and witnessed the storm high on the ridge above them. They knew deep down in their hearts that Gazali had had something to do with it, but weren't exactly sure what. After all, they had come to reclaim what was rightfully theirs, and nothing was going to deter them. There was only one thing they were certain of since they had arrived at the foot of the granite mountain, and that was, the nest was lying directly on top of the ridge above them. General Joe had spotted it in the distance with his telescope, just before their mode of transport lost altitude.

Ajani was busy filing his talons with a rasp, having chipped them on the jagged shards of granite. His thieving magpies were now starting to chill out. Cedric, joking apart said, "I'm glad that's all over!" with a glazed expression across his face.

"Phew, me too!" added Boyce, adjusting his eye patch

to a more comfortable position. He wiped the droplets of sweat from his feathered brow with the corner of his handkershute.

"Why do you wear an eye patch Boyce?" asked Jalen innocently.

"Because I want to look like a pirate," Boyce retorted with a wry grin.

"Do you think I would make a good pirate Boyce? Will you teach me?" asked Jalen in reply.

"That's no, to both questions!" answered Boyce, abruptly, giving Jalen a nasty frown, "that's Chad's job."

"I've got one more question, Boyce," Jalen said, feeling slightly nervous by Boyce's ugly expression.

"What's that?" answered Boyce, with an exasperated tone.

"Why do you carry a handkershute?" asked Jalen.

"I always like to be prepared for anything," Boyce replied, as he turned his back on Jalen and started to walk away from him.

Chad was nibbling scraps of meat. In between mouthfuls, he and Jalen were quietly shooting the breeze together. Jalen then began practicing his balancing skills. Boyce was tucking into a platter of mixed entrails, and Buzz was still lying in his hammock asleep, it was what he did best.

Cedric sauntered nervously over to join Ajani by the nest. He began ticking off the inventory of jewels, making sure that Gazali had not stolen anything that he shouldn't have.

"Not a bad attempt at a fake egg!" exclaimed Cedric, trying to sound enthusiastic by sucking up to his leader.

"Which one? His, or ours?" snapped Ajani, giving Cedric the evil eye.

"Well, ours of course. If it fooled him, it could fool

anyone," retorted Cedric, dropping his stone tablet on the ground.

"Hmmmmm," replied Ajani, who wasn't really listening. He was distracted and far too busy admiring his filed toenails. Ajani caught a glimpse of his reflection in the cracked glass of his broken fob watch. He opened his beak wide and poked his tongue out.

"That's a healthy colour," he exclaimed, waggling it about, and smacked his beak together in anticipation of a tasty platter of meat.

Neither Ajani, nor his magpie servants had been expecting what was going to happen next.

The storm clouds had dissipated, and the warm ultra violet rays from the sun re-emerged, exacerbating the stench from above. General Joe and the rescue party were as ready as they were going to be under the circumstances.

"We have to pounce now," said General Joe, "everybody knows what they have to do! Any further questions?" he asked, as he started to rummage around in his kit bag and distribute the arsenal of weapons to his pals.

Rafe was given the stun gun and a tiny fob watch. Roxy had her naturally spiked arms, that could be used as lethal weapons if required. Hugo had been given a catapult with small stones to use as ammunition. Guy had a bag of nails and left over banana skins. Zena had been given the rope ladder, which she slung over her shoulder, ready to place in position at the top of the ridge. General Joe set the trap net at the foot of the ridge. "Just in case there might be a chance of taking prisoners," he said, then showed Seth, being the eldest, how to engage the blunderbuss with his two rubber bullets.

"If you run out of ammunition you can always use your nuts in an emergency." General Joe exclaimed.

Seth, feeling somewhat defenceless retorted,

"I'll have to blag it if necessary. I have never used one of these before," he said, eyeing the gun up and down. Seth took up his post and stood on sentry duty by the trap net, watching and waiting with his chums.

General Joe then addressed his companions.

"Time waits for no man. Synchronize your watch Rafe. Kick off in fifteen minutes. This is how it was done in the old days. Time to get into position everybody. Rendezvous back here when the task is done. Off you go and good luck," he said.

Rafe and Guy dispatched themselves round to the eastern side of the mountain. They stealthily made their way to the top of the rocky crag, noticing that Gazali was nowhere to be seen. They were to wait for zero hour, then launch into action by creating a diversion.

The time had come. At the base of the ridge Roxy handed Hugo the canvas rucksack containing their replica egg. She gave it to Hugo, who slung it over his shoulder in preparation to climb up the rock face, using the rope ladder.

As Roxy stood at the base of the ridge and looked upwards to the top of the rock face in front of her, she knew she was born to carry out this task.

"This is right up my street!" Roxy declared.

Roxy was a brilliant climber and had to go up first. She elongated her body upwards, keeping her petal coated roots firmly dug in to the moist ground. She stretched her limbs to maximum length, clinging on to every nook and cranny that she could grab hold of, just stopping short of the top. From high up here Roxy took in the landscape. She could see the calm shimmering sea twinkling in the sunlight. Roxy then became aware of a foul stench from something nasty that she did not recognize. It was wafting from on top of the ridge above her. She held her nose for a moment to catch her breath. Roxy continued growing to the top, stopping just below the two dead tree stumps that were growing horizontally out of the side of the rock face.

General Joe, Seth and Zena were watching from below.

When Roxy had got to the top, she gave the buds up signal to Zena.

Zena began to scale her thorny arms, and trod on one of Roxy's sharp thorny spikes with her foot.

"OUCH!" she cried, quickly removing her foot in a natural reflex action.

Roxy quickly got her two pence worth in, never failing to seize an opportunity.

"CAREFUL! Why don't you look where you are going?" Roxy whined.

"Like you, you mean, when you burst the hot air Loon balloon," Zena retorted.

"That is SO unfair. You know it was an accident!"

Roxy exclaimed in her defense.

Zena, having lost the battle of words with Roxy, continued to scale her limbs. She was careful not to prick any of her feet again. She reached the top and let the rope ladder loose, keeping hold of the ends to tie them to the tree stumps with plant twine. Zena had to make sure it would be strong enough to support the weight of Hugo. It didn't take too long before she was soon retreating back down to the base of the ridge, shouting, "Careful as she goes!" with Roxy following close behind her.

It was now Hugo's turn. He gingerly put his foot on the bottom rung of the rope ladder, making sure it would take his weight. Hugo proceeded to climb upwards to the halfway mark. From this vantage point he would wait for the signal from General Joe to complete his mission, being careful to remain out of sight.

Rafe and Guy were now in position on the eastern side of the ridge. They hid behind a large granite boulder on the apex of the ridge, with three minutes to go till zero hour. While they waited they were busy weighing up the opposition, when Rafe pointed in the direction of three of the thieving magpies.

"Guy, look at them! You to tackle those three and I will go for the vulture, Ajani," declared Rafe.

"PHEW! Look at the size of him," added Guy, pointing at Chad, and daunted by the prospect of wrestling with him. There was a moment of thoughtful silence.

"I hope that there is no more of them," said Guy, "and what about the baby magpie over there?" he asked.

"He is too small to worry about. Look, he can barely fly," Rafe said, inhaling a breath of the foul air, "there is a horrible smell coming from somewhere."

They were both quietly watching. Guy crept forward from behind the granite boulder and gently sprinkled his nails on the ground, scattering them as far as possible, then tossed the banana skins after them, desperately trying not to attract attention.

Ajani and the magpie warriors were temporarily preoccupied with preening, and never even looked up.

Rafe and Guy were confident that they had got away with the first part of the operation unnoticed.

"That'll make them dance, and it should slow them down somewhat!" exclaimed Guy, smirking at the thought.

"Now remember Guy, don't hurt the baby!" said Rafe, "he is far too young to be part of all of this."

"Ok, I'll try not to," Guy retorted, compassionately.

They had both been waiting in anticipation for the fob watch to strike zero hour.

The fob watch chimed, 'DING, DING, DING.'

"That's the signal. Here goes!" said Rafe, "This is it, over the top, as the General would say."

Guy thrust forward to lure the magpies away from Rafe in his direction, to where the nails and banana skins lay in wait. Rafe lunged forwards from their temporary hiding place and 'ZAPPED' Ajani with his stun gun.

Feeling the full force from the impact of Rafe's weapon, Ajani let out the most unimaginable piercing scream. His body writhed as he twisted and turned to try and fight back, whilst attempting to get out of the way of the electrifying rays that were scorching his feathers. Ajani was powerless as his stiff rigid body finally toppled over sideways, landing on the nest and covering its contents. He was at last, out cold.

* * *

General Joe, with his chums Seth, Zena and Roxy could hear the commotion up above them.

"Hugo has very strong arms and legs for this sort of escapade," said Seth, propping the blunderbuss on his left shoulder and leaning it against the side of his ear.

Hugo ascended to the top of the rocky crag with the rucksack over his shoulder. He inhaled a whiff of the foul air coming from on top of the ridge. He had his catapult with small stones in his trouser pocket; that could and would be fired if necessary. He lay in wait like a fox in his lair, ready to pounce on the General's signal, when he heard Rafe shouting.

"OH NO!" cried Rafe, as he ran towards Guy, waiting

further over on the ridge, "That's torn it! He's fallen onto the nest, and covered the egg. Let's get out of here. There is nothing more we can do. It's up to Hugo now."

The two of them beat a hasty retreat back down the ridge, to rendezvous with the rest of the rescue party.

* * *

The magpies didn't know which way to go first. Should they chase after these two escaping menaces, or help Ajani. But in their hurry to go over to assist Ajani, the magpie warriors trod on the nails that had been scattered by Guy, and were screeching,

"OOH, OUCH, OOH, OUCH!" as they danced about in circles, hopping from one foot to the other like cats on a hot tin roof.

Chad had managed to usher Jalen back into the entrance of the cave out of harm's way, then re-emerged, and *"BOOF,"* slipped on a banana skin. He got his wings in a twist as he lost his balance completely.

"AAHHHH!" Chad yelled, skidding wildly out of control. He was now on his tail feathers heading for the edge of the ridge. His speed was such, that he left claw marks in his wake, but managed to put his breaks on, just in time to stop himself from going over the edge.

"Phew, that was close!" Chad said. He quickly recovered his dignity, and stuck his split tail feathers upwards in a final act of defiance, to whoever was watching.

Boyce was in big trouble too. He had nails in one claw, and was sliding on a banana skin with the other. He was swirling round and round on one leg, like a spinning top out of control.

"YIKES, HEEEELP!" Boyce bellowed. He came to an

abrupt halt, crashing head on into the rock wall and displacing his eye patch. Boyce felt the full force of his body weight trying to overtake him, and ended up on the ground, upside down, and unable to get up in this stupefied state. As he lay in a heap, propped up against the granite rock, he saw stars spinning round his head with his whirling eyes.

Cedric stood there dazed by what was going on around him. "What shall I do first? Should I help Ajani? Should I go after those two escaping menaces, or should I stay and protect the genuine egg inside the cave? After all, are those subordinates really worth risking life and limb for?"

* * *

Finally, from the base of the ridge General Joe gave the signal, "Time to crack on Hugo, over you go!" he shouted.

Hugo having heard the General's order, surreptitiously peered over the top and saw the nest. A disturbing sight confronted him, with Rafe and Guy nowhere to be seen. "UH!" he gasped, noticing that Ajani was out cold directly in front of him. The smell from his scorched feathers reminded him of burnt bar-be-que fish. Hugo looked down toward General Joe who was still waiting at the foot of the rock face with Seth, Roxy and Zena.

"Ajani has fallen over on to the nest, I cannot access the egg," he bellowed.

"What do you mean you cannot access the egg? You'll have to! Put your hand underneath him and ease it out Hugo," the General shouted in reply.

Hugo didn't fancy the idea of rummaging around

under Ajani's tail feathers, but he knew that everybody was depending on him, so there would be no backing out now.

"Well, I guess life's a slice," said Hugo, as he gingerly put one hand in, clinging on for dear life with the other to the rope ladder. He felt around in the nest for the shape of the egg. Ajani's weight was incredibly heavy, as he lay motionless. Hugo eventually found the egg shape under the tail feathers.

"I HAVE GOT IT!' Hugo shouted, prizing it out from beneath the unconscious vulture.

Hugo cautiously placed it in the rucksack, and removed his replica egg from the bag, being very careful not to mix them up. He then forced his replacement egg into the nest.

"Time to get out of here!" Hugo said, "Hopefully, Ajani will never know the difference."

Having recovered the precious cargo, Hugo began his descent, carrying the booty over his shoulder. He stepped off the bottom rung of the rope ladder, and passed the bag to Zena to look after.

* * *

As the magpie servants recovered, they were feeling extremely vexed, confused and exhausted. It had been a very trying day. First, Gazali's performance, and now this, it was all too much. For one thing, they were thirsty from all the acrid smoke they had inhaled into their lungs, and their eyes were still streaming from it, and to cap it all they had had only time to eat snacks.

As Boyce regained his senses he called out to Cedric, "They've gone over the edge. Look, over there," he said, pointing towards the sheer drop.

Cedric had been far too hesitant. By the time he had decided which way to go and what to do, it was all over.

"It's far too late now, it's only the replica anyway, not that they know that," retorted Cedric, in an attempt to justify his actions, feeling somewhat overwhelmed.

Rafe and Guy had now rejoined the other members of the rescue party.

"Did you get it Hugo?" asked Guy.

"Yes, we have it," Hugo replied.

"We got off lightly there Guy," declared Rafe.

"It was easier than I thought it would be," said Guy, "and those banana skins and nails were a brilliant idea. The chaos was fantastic," he said, smiling at the recollection of seeing Chad and Boyce lose control.

* * *

Cedric reluctantly went over to see Ajani, feeling nervous in his stomach. He knew Ajani would be less than impressed at what had happened. Ajani was slowly coming round. The black baseball cap on his head was skew-whiff. His feathers were badly ruffled and scorched around the edges. Ajani was wobbly on his talons as he attempted to get up. It was not a good sign of things to come.

"Errh, what happened?" Ajani asked curiously, in an abrupt manner.

"You were hit by a stun gun, sir," Cedric replied nervously.

"A stun gun! No wonder I've got a headache," retorted Ajani, still feeling totally stupefied. He was trying to refocus his dark cruel eyes on his surroundings.

"Yes sir," said Cedric softly, trying not to aggravate the situation further, "you were."

Boyce and Chad removed the sharp piercing nails from their claws. Chad went into the cave to fetch the feather broom to sweep the nails into a pile, to be disposed of later. Boyce attempted to remove the offending banana skins, and had thrown them to one side for nibbles later, not looking where he had tossed them.

"Mm, tasty snacks for tonight," said Boyce, "looking forward to those, got to keep up with this five a day lark!" he said, with a grin across his face.

Ajani was still in a state of semiconsciousness. He composed himself just enough to be able to turn his head to peer over the cliff edge to see the Gurglewobblers, Orchids and Flower people making their escape. As he tried to stand upright he wobbled on his talons, and he unknowingly took a step backwards towards the edge. Chad, Boyce and Cedric cried, "LOOK OUT!" all at the same time. There was an almighty *'BOOMPH.'*

"OOH, OUCH, AAAAAH!" Ajani cried out with an ear splitting screech. Too late, he had slipped base over apex on one of the banana skins, landing on his already crumpled and scorched tail feathers. To cap it all he had trodden on a nail that had been missed by Chad with the feather broom during the sweeping up, and it was piercing his toe.

Cedric couldn't bear to look and pulled the brim of his hat down to cover his eyes.

"That's blown it!" exclaimed Cedric, as a sickening nervous feeling came over him, right down to the pit of his stomach.

Ajani gave them all an evil glare. He opened his bill to maximum stretch.

"YOU, YOU, AND YOU, SCRAM!" Ajani screamed, as he lunged towards each and every one of his servants in turn, narrowly missing them with his lethal beak.

Cedric, Chad and Boyce belted off double quick, shaking with apprehension back into the cave, leaving their leader clearly in a state of unimaginable rage.

Ajani knew in the back of his mind that they had not heard the last of this, when both parties realize they have a replica egg, they will both be back.

* * *

Meanwhile the General and his companions were making a dash for it. Luckily for Seth, he had not needed to use the blunderbuss, let alone the rubber bullets or his nuts, and Hugo had not had the chance to use his catapult.

"Time to leave everybody, our task is over," said Hugo, as he hastily helped to gather the remnants of the equipment together.

General Joe was feeling very proud of his team. "Well done, all of you, you have all shown great courage today," he said.

Seth was single-handedly attempting to roll up the trap net.

"Seth, no time for that, leave it there with the rope ladder. Now let's head for home," declared General Joe.

Once they had left the danger zone, they stopped and ate the left over egg sandwiches and washed them down with plenty of water, then rested their weary legs for a little while.

"Can I see the egg, please?" asked Seth, looking directly at Zena.

"Here Seth, take it," Zena said, feeling happy to unload the precious cargo. She brushed down the long flowing leaves of her outfit with her hands, then used

General Joe's magic tonic to clean the wound on her foot before sticking a plaster on it.

Seth opened the rucksack and quickly peeped inside.

"Well it looks genuine," he said, as he closed the bag, and put it over his shoulder.

"All's well that ends well!" said Seth, looking down at his dirty boots. "These need a polish, and I could do with a lovely revitalizing cup of honey and nettle tea."

"I'm afraid you'll have to wait for that Seth," General Joe replied.

The rescue party had not realized for one moment that Seth was carrying Gazali's replica egg. After all, it was a perfect copy.

It was time to press on, and the rescue party walked back under the canopy of trees in the direction of the hot air balloon. They had all risen to the challenge on the day, and were feeling, quite rightly, extremely proud of themselves and their victory.

The air, although humid and stifling, was so much sweeter here. They could hear the familiar sound from the insects buzzing in the vast undergrowth, as they went about the daily business of survival, completely oblivious to the events of the day.

Seth was thinking how proud his ancestors would be of this victory against damnation. How brave Hugo and Guy had been, not forgetting the part that they had all played in the recovery of this precious jewel.

General Joe was used to such skirmishes, and delighted that his companions had carried off such a successful feat without a hitch.

Hugo, Rafe and Guy were busy exchanging details of their engagement, while Roxy and Zena were chatting over next year's fashions, all the way back to the balloon.

* * *

Jalen had been watching the fiasco from inside the cave.

"What's going on out there?" Buzz asked Jalen from his hammock.

"Oh, you should have seen it. It was so funny," replied Jalen, turning round and talking to Buzz.

"What was?" asked Buzz.

Jalen had to explain to Buzz what had happened, using hand signals to demonstrate as he spoke.

"The Mystic Gazali made a big storm and stole what he thought was the real jewelled egg, replacing it with his own replica and escaped. Everyone thought that the robbery was over for the day when the Orchids, Flower people, and the Gurgle something or others turned up, and knocked out Ajani with a stun gun, frazzling his feathers and stealing Gazali's replica egg. Chad and Boyce then slipped over on banana skins and trod on some nails, it was utter chaos. Cedric didn't know which way to turn first, and in the end was no help to anybody. The thing is, everybody thinks that they have the genuine egg, but nobody has, do they Buzz?"

Buzz was having difficulty keeping up. "Don't they?" he answered, with a quizzical look.

"No, silly, the real egg is hidden in this cave," answered Jalen.

"Yeah right, I knew that," retorted Buzz, somewhat surprised, and hoping to get away with the fact that he had no idea.

Buzz was starting to feel a little bit better now.

"It looks like I'm missing all the action," he said.

"You sure are!" Jalen answered, fluttering around the cave, unsuccessfully practicing his flying skills.

"Pass me my crutch," said Buzz, "I'm getting up."

Jalen went over to the far corner of the cave and dragged Buzz's crutch over for him.

"Here Buzz," Jalen said, passing it to him.

Buzz gently slid out of his hammock, and stood up with the aid of his crutch to help support him, still unaware of what lay beneath him, and Jalen still never told him.

"You're a mess Buzz!" Jalen exclaimed.

"Well, I guess I have felt better. Now let's see what all the fuss is about," Buzz retorted, as he and Jalen slowly made their way to the entrance of the cave and peeped outside.

"Core blimey, what a mess. It looks like a battlefield! I'm sure it's got something to do with the seven years bad luck that the broken mirror brings with it," Buzz exclaimed.

Cedric, Boyce and Chad saw Buzz coming.

"Thanks for your help, pal!" said Chad sarcastically, looking Buzz straight in the eye.

"What help?" asked Buzz.

"Exactly!" they all shouted together, turning to look at him.

"UH!" said Buzz, "What did I do?" asked Buzz, not understanding the comment.

"Nothing, that's the point," they all said together in unison.

Chad wandered over to the cliff edge and hoisted up the rope ladder left behind by the now departed raiders. He decided to leave the trap net in place, as it could prove useful to them in the future. If anyone trod on it, they would be scooped up and left swinging in the breeze.

It was now late afternoon and Ajani was lying by his nest. He was still smouldering with the emotions of

R.A.F. (revenge, anger and frustration).

"Two robberies in one day, unbelievable, that's part of my nest egg in tatters!" Ajani declared.

Cedric carefully tiptoed up behind Ajani and placed a platter of bangers and buffalo chips quietly on the ground, startling Ajani. Cedric jumped backwards with fright as Ajani turned on him, still raging, pecking and lunging at him with his deadly bill. Cedric was hot to trot to get out of the way and ran towards his thieving comrades for protection.

Cedric thought that because the day had been fraught with so much danger all round, it was now time for him and his birds to party. Cedric went into the cave and promptly returned with supplies of sweet meats for their feast. When eaten, they glided down the back of the throat like crunchy dormant earwigs.

Jalen and Buzz were playing a game of marbles with their nuts, while Chad and Boyce fetched the Adams Ale from the back of the cave for their quaffing contest.

Gazali the Projectile

CHAPTER 14

THE GREAT ESCAPE

Gazali and Jupitor were long gone. They were speeding along homeward bound, back to the Mystic Mountains as fast as Jupitor's sturdy legs could carry them. Jupitor was making the most of the wind blowing through his sandy mane. The sweet smell of honeysuckle and lavender cleared his nostrils of the foul stench from the Aolian Mountains, and as far as he was concerned, the sooner they returned home the better.

Gazali was feeling victorious and thought he had been very clever in the execution of his plan to grab this precious cargo. His controlled weather storm had ceased, along with the lightening and thick acrid smoke, and he was making his escape with the warmth of the sunshine on his back.

"It is no more than I deserve!" Gazali mused to himself.

Jupitor was galloping so fast that Gazali's large bulging red lip wobbled from the G-force.

"Hurry Jupitor, hurry, we must be home before nightfall!" Gazali said, egging him on.

"Tell me about it, I'm going as fast as I can!" said Jupitor sarcastically, "and I can't see very well in the dark."

"Eat more carrots then, my dear boy, eat more

carrots," retorted Gazali, knowing full well that Jupitor hated carrots.

Gazali had no idea that he had taken possession of an imitation egg. He was completely unaware that the rescue party had swapped their egg for his replica. He had hidden what he believed was the genuine egg on the back of his cart, and covered it over with a tartan green blanket that his father had given him all those years ago.

"I knew it would come in handy for something one day," he mused.

* * *

General Joe and his search party had at last made it back safely to their hot air balloon. Everybody was in exceedingly good high spirits and looking forward to going home. Zena and Roxy were looking forward to cooling their heels in the damp nutritious soil, and imbibing in some of Kiandra's fortifying home-made herbal tonic. They all bundled themselves into the basket, and Seth secured the precious cargo tightly over his shoulder in preparation for lift off.

"Cast off," Hugo shouted.

Up they went, high into the troposphere. The breeze had changed direction from a northerly to a southwesterly. It was the perfect wind direction for the Valley of the Gems, though they would be carried slightly more inland.

As they were gliding through the sky like a bird on the wing, they enjoyed the warm delicious breeze that blew round them like a swirling dervish. They were flying at great speed, high above the treetops and Rafe exclaimed, "Look at that magnificent view!"

Seth observed that Roxy was about to stretch her long thorny arms to point skyward.

"No, Roxy, keep your arms down, we don't want to repeat your earlier performance," Seth shouted.

Roxy, still feeling awkward, looked down to the ground below them. She had spotted a blue orchid and a large horse galloping at great speed.

"LOOK, DOWN THERE!" she exclaimed, pointing eastward.

"By Jove, that's Gazali," General Joe said, pulling out his telescope from his kit bag for a better look.

Gazali and Jupitor were going so fast that the green tartan blanket had blown back on one corner of the cart, revealing a glimpse of what looked like a jewelled egg, and it was clear to see.

"Heavens above, he's got an egg!" exclaimed General Joe, somewhat astonished.

"So what have we got?" asked Seth rhetorically.

"The real one or a fake one?" asked Zena.

"I don't know now," General Joe replied disappointedly.

"There is only one thing for it. We had better take Gazali's egg too, just in case," said Guy.

"How are we going to do that from here, when he is going at that speed?" asked Rafe.

"Simple," said Zena, "We'll use the grab claw."

"Sounds like a plan," declared Guy, rubbing his hands together with glee.

"I need a hero!" General Joe exclaimed, pointing at Hugo.

"IT'S RUDE TO POINT GENERAL. ANYWAY, WHY ME? IT'S ALWAYS ME!" retorted Hugo, throwing his arms upwards toward the sky.

"That's settled then, unanimous vote, Hugo to go!"

said Seth, wanting to play a trick on him for pinching his 'thinking cap' yesterday.

"What do you mean unanimous vote? I never saw any voting. What happened to democracy?" stated Hugo.

"Oh, that doesn't exist here. It's a bit like death and taxes, which is the only thing that is sure in mortal life. Anyway, enough of that, we have nominated you for the task," retorted General Joe.

Hugo did not quite understand the General's remark, and gave him a quizzical look.

"OKAY, OKAY, YOU WIN, I'LL GO!" said Hugo, feeling like a martyr, and knowing full well that he was not going to win the argument.

"The grab claw is not long enough to reach the egg from this height. We need to get much closer," General Joe said looking at his companions.

They began to lower the Loon balloon. Zena clasped the grab claw from General Joe's kit bag and handed it to Hugo.

"Hugo, you slide down the safety rope with the grab claw and GRAB IT. It's that simple," ordered General Joe.

Hugo was remembering his escapades earlier dangling on the end of a rope, and did not want to repeat the performance. His buttocks were still stinging from where the branches of the treetops twanged his hindquarters, plus his hands were still sore from his rope burn. Hugo reluctantly clambered over the edge of the basket clutching hard onto the long rope. He proceeded to slide down to the end, swinging in the breeze like a pendulum. When he got to the bottom, he took the grab claw from his pocket while holding on to it tightly.

"LOWER AND CLOSER!" Hugo shouted, hanging on single-handedly for dear life.

They all did their best to manoeuvre the Loon balloon to the rear of the cart. They were closing in, avoiding the treetops. Hugo had to remove the blanket first. He was nearly there. The grab claw was swinging around all over the place, in every which direction imaginable. As he approached the target at full stretch of his body and arm, he managed to pull the blanket off. It blew back and covered his face, obscuring his vision. For a moment Hugo looked like a green tartan ghostly figure on a haunting. He quickly brushed the blanket aside and watched as it floated down towards the ground out of the way, exposing the jewelled egg in all its glory.

Gazali sensing that something was happening behind his back, turned his head round to take a peep.

"WHOA!" he shouted to Jupitor.

Jupitor immediately stopped dead in his tracks as the cart concertinaed into his hindquarters. The force from the impact of the collision shuffled Jupitor forwards, catapulting Gazali off his seat, head first, flying through the air like a missile. He saw his own reflection looking back at him when his crystal ball overtook him at great speed. They both together, subsequently crashed into a tree. Gazali unceremoniously slumped to the ground in a heap, feeling stunned. He was once again reunited with his crystal ball. The tips of his moustache had found their way up each of his two nostrils. The stars above his head were spinning round like whizzing Catherine wheels before his eyes. His blue silk robe lay crumpled beyond recognition around his scrawny battered body.

Hugo seized the moment and lurched forward with the grab claw and seized the egg.

"GOT IT, QUICK, HOIST ME UP, NOW!" Hugo bellowed.

Hugo was promptly pulled back inside the wicker

basket with the second precious cargo. Once safely on his feet, he put the second egg in Seth's bag next the other one.

"Quick! Time to get out of here! I never thought we would be saying that again today!" exclaimed Rafe.

They made a dash for it, for the second time that day. The rescue party took the Loon balloon to a higher altitude. They needed to go in the opposite direction to escape Gazali and the Aolian Mountains, homeward bound A.S.A.P.

As they left the scene they looked down to the ground and could see that Gazali was still flat on his back, stupefied, and left him to it. There was absolutely no chance of taking him prisoner from this altitude.

On the ground Jupitor's hindquarters were still shuddering from yet another one of life's nasty experiences. "Typical, stupid man, this is like the butt kicking from hell!" he said, rolling his eyes upwards in disgust, looking at his master.

The rescue party were now well on their way home to the Valley of the Gems. They settled down in the basket as best they could. Hugo was the hero of the moment, again. He had shown great courage and bravery as always.

"Well, let me see!" General Joe mused. He took both the eggs out of Seth's bag and held them in the palms of his hands.

"Gazali must have swapped this egg for a fake one. We then swapped Gazali's fake egg for our replica, therefore, this one must be the genuine article," said General Joe with confidence.

"It sounds like a logical deduction, but I'm confused. Does that mean that we have scooped a real coup?" asked Hugo.

"We won't be able to tell which one is the real egg until we get back to the Valley of the Gems, they are both identical," said Seth taking them from the General and packing them securely away in his rucksack.

"Mm! That all seems to make perfect sense," Seth exclaimed.

It was getting late and the sun was going down in the Valley of the Gems. Queen Kohana was now becoming very anxious for the safety of the rescue party.

"They should have been back by now," she said, musing to herself. Had they been successful? Was anyone hurt, or worse? How would they react to the news of Artie's betrayal? She looked skyward and in the distance saw a small red orb approaching, and said, "Thank goodness, what a relief."

She gathered the inhabitants of the forest together to welcome the rescue party home. Kiandra and Leo lit the homemade candles to mark out the landing strip for them to aim at.

At last they landed safely down on terra firma with huge cheers all round. Livia had put the kettle on to make Seth's favourite brew of honey and nettle tea for him and all the Gurglewobblers, and Kiandra rushed forward with her homemade nectar for Rafe, Zena and Roxy.

The basket was unloaded. When they had finished their drinks, Livia looked down at Seth's boots, "They're filthy Seth, you always told me that one can judge a person's character by the state of their shoes!" she said with a beaming smile across her face.

"Yes, I know Livia, but we have been rather preoccupied today, my dear," replied Seth, looking distinctly shattered.

"Has anyone seen my two rubber bullets, I appear to

have lost them?" Seth asked, looking away from Livia.

"Oh, I'm sure they will turn up Seth. We will have a good look for them later," answered the General.

"Welcome back all of you," said Queen Kohana, as she approached the rescue party with a puzzled expression upon her face, "I see that you have acquired two precious cargos."

Seth and General Joe explained what had happened, informing her that Gazali had turned traitor. She was horrified.

"There is more bad news I'm afraid. Artie had met a magpie named Cedric a few days earlier in the forest while out walking on the trail. He had been tricked into telling the magpie about the existence of the egg. It was Talia and Livia that had overheard him talking to Banjo about what had happened," said Queen Kohana.

"Where is he now?" enquired Seth.

"Elie is guarding Artie and Banjo over there, in the first of the two mines," answered the queen.

"We need to find out which one of these eggs is genuine," interrupted Rafe.

Roxy and Zena fetched the two eggs from the large rucksack in the basket, and took them into the mine to where the Amrit crystal base was situated. Everybody followed Roxy and Zena into the mine. The eager expectation amongst the rescue party was indescribable. They passed Artie and Banjo as they went by, giving them a sideways glance, not stopping to acknowledge them. Artie and Banjo felt like the earth would swallow them up, and decided that it if there was a moment to be quiet, this was it.

Seth took over from Roxy. Seth and Zena stepped forward into the light beam that radiated through the hole in the ceiling of the mine, and placed the precious cargo on to the Amrit crystal base. They waited with bated breath. Nothing happened.

"It must be the other one then!" exclaimed Zena.

They swapped the eggs over and waited with equal expectation, and couldn't understand why nothing happened again.

"Two replica eggs," General Joe stated while scratching his moustache, "IMPOSSIBLE!"

It was jaw dropping, everybody gasped. They had risked life and limb for *this*.

"Not forgetting the egg we placed into Ajani's nest," piped up Roxy.

"That makes three now," Rafe chipped in.

There was a stony silence, as they all looked at each other in disbelief.

Artie and Banjo had been quietly listening, and were as shocked as everyone else. Whilst they had been left on their own, they had been conspiring together whilst sitting by the entrance of the mine.

"WE'VE GOT AN IDEA," they shouted together enthusiastically.

"You two have done enough damage already," Seth retorted with a stern glare.

"NO, NO, LISTEN, PLEASE," Artie squealed.

"We are all ears," declared Rafe.

Everybody gathered around, and Artie with the help of Banjo explained the idea to everybody.

"It's not that ridiculous," General Joe declared, giving their suggestion consideration.

"So far we have got away without being attacked from the north. But we must keep our guard up here, as we are not out of the woods yet," said Queen Kohana.

"Who is to go with you General?" the Queen asked.

"I will get back to you on that one, Your Majesty,"

replied General Joe, "just give me a little time to think the idea through."

"How much time do you need?" asked Hugo.

"How long is a piece of string?" retorted Guy mockingly.

"What about that traitor, Gazali?" enquired Livia.

"Now, now, relax everybody, I didn't get where I am today by getting in a panic. I'll sleep on it, and I suggest that you all do the same. We will talk again in the morning," said the General.

The large parish lantern shone like a silver rosette illuminating the forest floor, as the stars twinkled like diamonds in the black night sky. It was now time for bed. The orchids scrambled to the top of their tenement treetops, to stay high and dry under a canopy of leaves. General Joe was pacing up and down outside his tent contemplating his next move as he inhaled the fresh night air, while the Flower people went back to their roots to dig their heels into the cool damp soil for the night.

Seth and Leo searched through all the equipment and bags for the two missing rubber bullets before turning in for the night. They were nowhere to be found and presumed lost for good.

"No point in worrying about it. It's too late," said Seth, walking away.

Seth and Leo went over to join the rest of their companions. The Gurglewobblers tucked themselves up for a night under the stars in their sleeping bags. The gentle aroma wafting up their nostrils from the lavender pillows that Elie and Kiandra had made, would ensure a good night's rest. They were glad this fraught day had come to a close, and just as they were drifting off to sleep;

"Look, there's a shooting star," said Leo.

"That's meant to be lucky," answered Talia.

"Quick, make a wish," piped up Livia.

"You must not tell anyone what it is," said Seth.

"Or it won't come true!" exclaimed Hugo and Guy together.

"What an adventure we have all had today," said General Joe mumbling quietly to himself.

They had all taken huge risks. The outcome had not been what they had all expected, but nonetheless, this was the way it had turned out.

Artie and Banjo had been allowed to leave the mine on the proviso that there would be no more nonsense. Their mother took them back to the stem and wrapped them up in her leaves for a goodnights sleep.

"Can we have a drink of your delicious home-made pollen juice before going to sleep, please mum?" asked Artie.

Darva went and fetched the brew.

"I knew you would want some of this. I have already made it. It should be nicely cooled down now for you both to drink," said Darva, handing them their beakers. They swallowed it down double quick, and Banjo had won this time.

"Yippee! Victory, I beat Artie!" Banjo exclaimed.

Darva began telling her twins a bedtime story about a young bee orchid that went for a walk in the forest, that had come across a stranger.

"Tomorrow is another day and I will finish the story then," Darva said, giving them both a goodnight kiss.

General Joe eventually settled down for the night. He too had seen the shooting star blaze across the cosmos and made his secret wish.

"That is a good omen!" he declared.

The General went inside his tent, removed his black

boots and slid into his sleeping bag.

"Maybe things would look better in the morning!" he mumbled to himself. The General drank his energizing herbal brew. As it slid down his lumpy pea-shooter, he felt the vitamin rush course through his veins.

"Ah, that's more like it!" he exclaimed, and was soon asleep.

CHAPTER 15

GAZALI RECOVERS

Gazali was still recovering from his hair-raising experience. It was the first time that he had ever been used as a projectile, and hopefully the last. It was something that he didn't enjoy or want to get used to.

"Well I guess that went to hell in a hand cart!" Gazali said, gathering his belongings together that lay sprawled across the landscape. He scooped up his crystal ball off the ground. As he gazed into this spherical orb he couldn't see into the future, only a message in writing, which read; "No signal, please contact your service provider." He mused for a moment. "Ooh, this is strange, I haven't seen this before."

Gazali straightened his shabby crumpled robe, then clambered back on to the wooden seat on his cart in readiness to leave.

"Jupitor, take me home now, if you please," he said.

Jupitor was still in a huff and feeling sarcastic as he spoke.

"This has been the butt kicking from hell," Jupitor said, as he nursed his sore battered haunches.

"What miles per hour would you like me to gallop at master, or should I say horse power? Nought to sixty in two seconds! Will that be fast enough for you?" asked Jupitor.

"Nice and slow please Jupitor, nice and slow," retorted Gazali, mopping his brow and still feeling rather shaken up after the trials and tribulations of the day.

"Blimey, I even got a please. He must be desperate. Manners maketh man, I suppose. But that doesn't necessarily apply to him," said Jupitor as he slowly accelerated away.

"I don't think we have heard the last of this, my trusty steed," said Gazali nervously.

"When those Gurglewobblers, Orchids and Flower people realize that my egg is an imitation, well, who knows what will happen next?" Gazali mused quietly to himself.

It was now getting late and the sun was starting to go down. It had been a very long day and Gazali had decided that they were to head straight for home, without taking respite on their journey.

Eventually in the distance Gazali could see the silhouette of the Mystic Mountains.

"Ah home sweet home," Gazali said, lighting his lantern.

It was not too long before they arrived at his hollowed out tree stump. "I am so tired after the day's events that I need to rest," said Gazali.

Jupitor was unharnessed and dumped in his cold dank cavern for the night. After his experiences of *this* day, it was a welcome relief to be in here talking to the fossils. At least they couldn't answer him back.

"I need my oats and water, master!" exclaimed Jupitor, clearing his throat of dust.

Gazali promptly gave Jupitor his staple diet of oats and sugar cubes with a bucket of water, closing the stable door behind him as he left.

Gazali was now ready for his feast of liquid fertilizer

by the quart, and settled down for the night, too weary even to look at his spell book.

As he lay down for the night he saw a shooting star blaze across the black velvety sky, and began quietly singing a song.

"Catch a shooting star, and put it in your pocket, save it for a rainy day."

Gazali got one last passing shot in before drifting off to sleep.

"So much for it bringing me luck, if it were not for bad luck, I wouldn't have any luck at all. Goodnight Jupitor, goodnight," he said.

CHAPTER 16

PLANNING

THE MATINÉE PERFORMANCE

"Dew on the grass, rain shan't pass!" exclaimed Seth to the General, who happened to be washing his face in the clear water of the stream. The early morning mist and dew disappeared to reveal a spectacular sunrise of sky blue pink, as the sun peeped through the cumulus clouds.

These two old bulldogs had the hearts of lions, and had risen very early before the rest of the inhabitants of the forest. The Gurglewobblers were still in the land of nod, fast asleep in their snug sleeping bags. The lavender pillows that Kiandra had made for them were obviously doing their job.

Seth and General Joe were busy discussing tactics, as they sat together on the grey stone bench. They were drinking a beaker of Seth's honey and nettle tea, while basking in the warm rays from the early morning sun.

"So what do you think of Artie and Banjo's idea?" Seth asked General Joe.

"Well, they do have a point, I suppose. If we decide to go with their idea, it would make Artie in particular feel that he had contributed to put right the terrible wrong that he had committed on his part," answered General Joe calmly.

"Banjo too, even though he was not directly involved," replied Seth.

"I hope they will both learn a lesson from this experience," replied the General.

"I agree," said Seth, topping up the Generals beaker with more honey and nettle tea.

During the debacle between them, they both agreed that they should take all the remaining arsenal of weapons with them.

"We have to be prepared!" remarked General Joe.

They had left the rope ladder and the trap net behind. Therefore because it remained in situ, it could still prove very useful, if it were still there.

"The burning question is, who shall accompany us on this mission?" asked General Joe.

"Apart from ourselves, Artie and Banjo. How about Hugo and Guy for starters? They are fearless and have shown great courage and bravery," said Seth, placing his beaker down on the ground and resting his elbows on his knees.

"So have all the others," answered General Joe, as he continued to speak.

"Every member of the rescue party has shown great camaraderie, determination and enthusiasm, which has been the driving force behind the campaign. I believe we need a pincer movement this time Seth. By that I mean that initially a larger search party shall go out together, and then we should divide into two smaller groups. Group one shall retrieve the precious cargo, and group two shall remain behind at the rendezvous point to bring us back. If we do not return within a specified time frame then group two will then be forced to step in and take over from group one," stated General Joe.

"Well, that does sound reasonable, I suppose,"

replied Seth, "I know that Talia would like to go. She is desperate to know what lies north of the valley. Personally I think she could do more good here."

"I'm inclined to agree with you Seth," retorted the General.

Seth had his 'thinking cap' on, and considered who would be best placed where, and doing what. Seth and General Joe eventually decided to keep the same group as before. They all worked so well together as a team. But they would also be taking Livia and Leo with them this time, for back up at the base camp.

"We are not even sure where the genuine egg is hidden, but you can be sure that the replica egg that we created will still be in Ajani's nest. There is only one other place that their's could possibly be, and that has to be inside the cave somewhere," said Seth.

General Joe paused for a moment while stroking his moustache.

"I have an idea to address that question," he said.

Once the General and Seth were satisfied that their strategy would work, and they both had to believe it would, they both approached the Queen together.

"May we speak with you, Your Majesty?" asked General Joe.

"Yes you may," Queen Kohana replied. "Come and be seated both of you," she said, indicating with the palm of her bud on the stone. The Queen was sipping her daily tonic from a jade cup.

"What is it?" she enquired.

"Both the General and I believe collectively, that we have come up with a workable strategy, Your Majesty. We would like to run the idea past you! And if you agree, we shall depart as soon as possible," said Seth.

Queen Kohana sat listening very attentively to both of

these experienced and wise elderly men, eventually agreeing with their idea in principle.

"Are you sure you can pull this off?" she asked them both, "we shall all be putting our trust in your hands."

"There are no guarantees, but it's all we've have at the moment, Your Majesty. If anything else arises we shall just have to think on our feet," said the General, glancing over to Seth for back up support.

"Who shall stay behind, and who shall accompany you?" asked Queen Kohana.

"Talia, Your Majesty has often dreamt of going north, but we both feel she would be more useful staying behind, but we should like to take Leo and Livia with us," said Seth.

The Queen thought for a moment, then answered Seth.

"Don't worry, I can find a special task for Talia that will make her feel invaluable here," she said.

Seth and General Joe were feeling jubilant between themselves that the queen had put her trust and confidence in both of them. All three of them agreed that it would be for the best to keep the names of the rescue party, and the details of their mission a secret for the time being.

Ajani on the Ridge

CHAPTER 17

HIGH ON AJANI RIDGE

The early morning condensation that hung over the Aolian Mountains like a veil, had now cleared to reveal the daystar. The warmth emanating from the ball of fire exacerbated the rancid stench from Ajani Ridge, as was usual for this time of the day.

Jalen was happily skylarking around, playing a game of hopscotch that Chad had taught him. Chad had told him that if he worked hard like a busy bee and stood on one leg to practice his balancing skills, he could perfect them.

"Practice makes perfect," Chad had told him, "and if you don't at first succeed, try, try, and try again."

Great words of wisdom Jalen thought. Jalen had a tendency to become overexcited and tried to run before he could walk. It was thirsty work doing this. Every now and again he paused to have a drink and eat some nuts or berries to keep him sustained. When consumed together the bitter concoction slid down his tiny gullet like treacle.

Inside the cave Buzz had got up. With the aid of his crutch that had been made by Chad and Jalen, Buzz was hopping about on one leg. He had decided not to join his chums for breakfast this morning. He had opted to take his nuts outside to split them open on the granite. Buzz gulped them down in such a frenzied attack, feeling the raw sensation scratching the back of his throat like a bucket full of nails.

Cedric was deep in thought sitting on his broken chair at his cruddy table. He had his breakfast with Chad and Boyce. They had imbibed on red berries, pieces of fatty rind, and anything else that they could find to enhance their feast.

Cedric began to express his concerns to his chums, as he picked at the leftovers.

"You do both realize that we have not heard the last of this, don't you?" said Cedric, "once Gazali, the Gurglewobblers, Orchids and Flower people put two and two together, they will be back. I'm sure of it."

Buzz entered the cave to rejoin his pals at the table.

"That makes four," said Buzz, with a smirk across his face, and feeling pleased that he had got his arithmetic correct.

"Oh do be quiet Buzz," said Cedric sharply.

"What did I do? I only did the sums," Buzz replied. He guzzled down some of Boyce's Adams Ale to clear the residue of nuts and shells that had got stuck in his throat.

"Pipe down Buzz," said Boyce, slightly irritated.

"If you can't say anything useful, don't say anything at all," said Cedric, putting his face right up close to Buzz's beak and scowling at him.

Buzz looked alarmed and recoiled back. He then walked over to study his reflection in the broken mirror.

"Mirror, mirror, on the wall, I'm the most good looking one of them all!" said Buzz in a moment of vanity. The mirror reflected back at him and shattered into a million pieces at the sound of his voice.

"Phew, that wasn't very nice!" exclaimed Buzz.

"So I guess we are in for another flipping seven years back luck. Mm! Now let me see. We already have seven years mapped out, minus the two years already gone, leaves five. Add on the extra seven years from this incident. That makes a total of twelve years left to go. Mm! The future, by all accounts doesn't look very bright does it?" he mused to himself.

Buzz picked up a small piece of stone to gouge out the extra lines into the wall, adjacent to Cedric's already recorded marks. It was now time for Buzz to scuttle back outside into the warm sun to watch Jalen's flying skills.

"Your flying skills have improved Jalen, you are getting very good," shouted Buzz, glad to be outside, "Have you had your breakfast yet?"

Jalen swooped down from the trees high above the ridge and landed directly in front of Buzz.

"Yes, I've eaten, and thankyou Buzz, that means a lot. Where is Chad?" Jalen asked.

"He's inside with the others, they are talking about something," answered Buzz.

Ajani had just about recovered from his ordeal of the previous day's events, but was still feeling tetchy and frazzled. He looked up from picking at the left over buffalo chips from the night before.

"WHATCHA UP TO, YOU TWO?" Ajani squawked. He began fluttering his bedraggled scorched wings up and down, and stretching his long scrawny neck in a display of authority.

Jalen, in all innocence tried to change the subject.

"Look at me Ajani. I can fly now, just like Chad," said Jalen proudly, attempting to show him what he could do.

"OKAY, SMARTY PANTS!" said Ajani in a gruff voice. "So you think you can fly do you? Well, I have a plan for YOU," he said, hopping round in circles on both talons, flapping his wings in excitement. Ajani lunged at Jalen, just missing him with his sharp hooked beak. Jalen froze on the spot, stiff rigid with fear.

Buzz and Jalen made eye contact, with a worried expression upon their faces. If Ajani had got a plan for Jalen, it could only be bad.

"FETCH THE OTHERS, NOW!" Ajani screeched at Buzz, as he straightened his black baseball cap.

Buzz limped over with the aid of his crutch, entering the cave to fetch Cedric, Boyce and Chad.

"He's so huffy puffy! Always huffy puffy! Phew! I dunno!" exclaimed Buzz to himself as he struggled on his good leg to hobble inside.

Jalen stood still on the spot, his claws still frozen to the ground and rigid with fear. His little heart was pounding like the beat of a big base drum. He had never done anything bad in his short life before, or hurt anyone. What would his mother say, if she knew? The thought of it made him shudder. So what on earth would Ajani require him to do?

Buzz shortly returned with Cedric, Boyce and Chad. The thieving magpies stood there silently waiting for their leader to speak, bracing themselves.

"Jalen is ready for his first mission," said Ajani staring straight into Jalen's eyes while posturing.

"UH!" gasped Jalen.

"He has been showing me his flying skills amongst other things. MOST IMPRESSIVE," Ajani snarled.

"I want you to send him on a dummy run, a 'recce,' and see how he gets on," said Ajani, "and bring me back a surprise, SOMETHING SHINY on your return," he snapped while playing to the gallery, "A nice jewel from the beach, or perhaps a pair of sunglasses that might enhance my image."

Jalen started to breathe normally again.

"Maybe I should disappear while I am at it," Jalen thought.

"He is far too small, sir," declared Chad, "although his training programme is progressing well, he is not ready for this kind of operation yet, SIR!"

Ajani arched his back fanning his feathers in a display of authority, while straightening his scrawny long neck. His dark black ruby eyes scowled at what stood before him as he opened his beak wide with rage to speak.

"YES HE IS! I WILL NOT HEAR ANOTHER WORD. NOW GET GONE, ALL OF YOU, OUT OF MY SIGHT!" he screamed, "OR I WILL CANCEL YOUR SCRAPS!"

It was the ideal opportunity for the magpie warriors to make a dash for it. Buzz in his hurry to get away tripped over a broken bone that was lying on the ground.

"Ouch. Ouch!" Buzz yelped, as he fell down to the ground, and rolling sideways like a puffball in motion.

Jalen rushed over and tried to push him back up onto his claws.

"You are far too big for me to handle Buzz!" declared Jalen.

Cedric carried on walking passed Buzz and went inside the cave, leaving Boyce and Chad to sort the fallen victim out; and where Buzz was concerned, there was always a mess left in his wake.

Chad and Boyce came over to help, picking up Buzz under his wings from the dusty granite floor and dragged him back inside, with Jalen following close behind shouting, "careful, careful!"

"Phew! He's in a really bad mood. Never any change there," said Buzz, referring to Ajani.

Chad and Boyce put Buzz back in his hammock and left him there.

Jalen went to lie down on the dirt floor exhausted, as the king-pins Cedric, Boyce and Chad stood around the shabby table debating what to do.

"I have the perfect answer," said Cedric to Chad and Boyce.

"We do need a lookout to tell us if anyone enters our kingdom. Jalen can fly high enough from branch to branch to be out of harm's way now. He can whistle to warn us of any impending subordinates," said Cedric, popping a handful of red berries into his mouth. As he sucked hard on the skins they burst forth like a citrus fountain, exploding on his tongue.

"I'm not so sure that he's up to it," Boyce said, guzzling back a cup of Adams Ale.

"He is quite capable," said Chad, "providing the branches are not too far apart, and he doesn't get over excited. You know what he can be like when he starts swooping all over the place and getting his plumage in a twist."

CHAPTER 18

SCHEMING GAZALI

Gazali had just about recovered from his previous ordeal of the day before. He was convinced that the shooting star he had seen last night would bring him good fortune on this bright new day. He had risked so much yesterday and had come home empty handed. "What a blow!" he said, as he scratched his itchy moustache, "I need to get the genuine egg back, and fast."

Jupitor was awake and poking his nose over his jagged stable door, taking in the sweet aroma of the lush pasture deep into his lungs. How refreshing it was after the stench of the north yesterday.

"Where's my breakfast, master?" Jupitor asked.

"What would you like this morning my dear friend, as a special treat?" asked Gazali, trying to cajole him along.

"I would normally ask for egg, master. But you appear to have got that all over your face yesterday!" replied Jupitor sarcastically.

"Oats it is then!" retorted Gazali abruptly, and promptly returned with them. He spoke to Jupitor as he began tipping the oats into the bag.

"The only idea I have come up with so far, is to perhaps travel to the Valley of the Gems, and try to convince everybody that I am not the traitor they all think I am, and perhaps we can retrieve the egg together, that may just work. What do you think to that, my old friend?" Gazali asked.

"Huh, I never heard such tosh in all my life. Besides, you *are* the traitor they all think you are," retorted Jupitor, "and in any case, I am in no mood to repeat yesterday's performance," he added, "I'm not budging."

"Great! Thwarted by a shire horse, just what I need right now!" declared Gazali as he stood swigging back his liquid tonic by Jupitor's stable door.

He left Jupitor on his own, hoping that his mood would improve, knowing that the chances of that were practically zero. Gazali walked back over to his hollowed out tree stump and sat down.

"Mm, I really must have that egg," he mused, "I really must have it."

CHAPTER 19

THE BOAT TRIP

"It's the perfect day for it!" exclaimed Seth, having already woken from his slumber and put his dusty boots on, "these will have to do!" he said, wiping the toes of his boots with the cuffs of his shirt to buff them up. He had forgotten to pack his shoe polish when they had left the Forest of Bark in such a hurry on that fateful morning. He relit the little dakota campfire for the second time that morning, and put the kettle on to boil.

"This is the best time of the day!" Seth remarked to the General.

Seth and General Joe were sitting next to each other on the small stone bench. Seth was telling the General his thoughts on how the balance of life and death is such a fine line, when the steam began billowing from the spout of the kettle like an erupting geyser.

"Ready for a cuppa?" asked Seth, as they sat chewing the cud together.

"Ooh, yes please," answered General Joe, "I've been looking forward to this."

General Joe and Seth sipped their tea while enjoying the warm sensation from the ultra violet rays of the sun on their backs. They were listening to nature's symphony from the dawn chorus. The General and Seth had been discussing their interview with the queen earlier in the day. They were both delighted that she had shown such confidence in their abilities, and were now looking forward to retrieving their precious cargo, once and for all. Both Seth and General Joe were experienced enough to realize that *this* day would be fraught with much danger.

Once Talia was up, Queen Kohana called her over and broke the news to her that she would not be going with the rescue party today.

"I have an equally important task for you to carry out here, along with Luella, Elie and Kiandra. We need your help with the organization for the protection of the forest and the Amrit crystal base. There may be an opportunity for you to travel out of the valley when these dark days are over. So I hope you will understand and not be too disappointed," said the Queen.

Talia cast her eyes downward to look to the earth beneath her feet.

"Very well Your Majesty," Talia replied. She began to role a tiny stone round in circles like a marble with the sole of her shoe.

"I am very flattered to be asked, and I am delighted to stay behind to help you all here," Talia retorted.

Deep down in her heart Talia felt it was such a bitter blow, and tried to lift her spirits. She was thinking about her cuckoo Pink's, and what he might be getting up to in her absence. Had he enough berries to eat? Would he be frightened of the dark? Would Austen look after him?

Moving her thoughts positively forwards Talia went to find Darva. Together they would set about making plenty of egg sandwiches and filling the flasks with fresh water for the rescue party to take with them. After all it was going to be a very long day for everybody.

General Joe and Seth felt it was now time to gather everyone down by the riverbank, as they were as ready as they were ever going to be. Once they had all assembled, General Joe made his announcement,

"I shall be in command of group one of the rescue party, and Seth shall be in command of group two. Group one shall be Hugo, Guy, Rafe, Zena, Banjo and Artie. We shall be laying the bait. Group two shall be Leo, Roxy and Livia who shall preside over the base camp with Seth in an area deemed safe upon arrival, and that is all I have to say for the moment. Is everybody ready?" he said.

There were cheers all round, "YES, we're ready!" they answered enthusiastically. There was a feeling of great optimism amongst everybody this morning.

Livia and Leo were secretly crossing their fingers behind their backs, hoping to be chosen, as they desperately wanted to be part of this plan, and were thrilled to be going. They were chuckling between themselves with delight.

"Grandma Gurgle would be very proud of me today. It is just as well that I still have my two red ribbons in my hair for double luck," Livia whispered into Leo's ear.

"Well, let's hope her superstitions are right. We are going to need all the luck we can get today!" retorted Leo, smiling at her. Although they both regretted Talia couldn't come. It didn't matter how large or small their part to play would be, it was just about being there, and doing something to help on this historical day.

"It is nearly time to go," said the General as he checked his kit bag for the very last time, using his inventory list,

"Baton, ah, most important," said General Joe, tucking it under his armpit. "Mallet, blunderbuss; We seem to have lost the two rubber bullets, but never mind,

156

we can use horse-chestnuts for ammunition instead; compass, magic tonic, extendable rope, survival guide book, four balls of string, camp fire making equipment, telescope, utensils for campfire 'just in case,' stun gun, fishing rod, large nails, two catapults, penknife, first aid kit, bow and arrows with rubber suckers. That should do it," he said.

The rope ladder and trap net were already there and the small nails had already been used up, so General Joe put an X next to them on the paper.

Darva and Talia had brought the egg sandwiches and liquid refreshments over, and gave them to Hugo and Leo to carry. The bananas and leftover cold cooked minted potatoes had been finished, devoured by Hugo and Guy at last night's feast. Hopefully there would be enough food here to sustain the rescue party for their journey.

The home guard gathered to wish their companions farewell, good luck and a speedy return.

"How are we going to transport all this kit, General?" asked Rafe.

"We shall be opting for shank's pony as far as the estuary, then from that point Seth has kindly agreed to allow us all to use the Gurglewobblers motor launch, *Moana*," replied the General, and for the second time that morning re-addressed all his companions together.

"If we use the Loon balloon again, Ajani along with his magpie warriors will see us coming, and that is what they will be expecting. I suspect they know that we will be returning at some point to reclaim what is rightfully ours. That is why we are going to travel in the motor launch to the north end of the coast, just south of the Bay of Vultures. From that point we shall execute Artie and Banjo's plan," announced General Joe.

Farewell to the Rescue Party

Darva stepped forward in a fluster, "You will take care, all of you, won't you?" she said to Seth and General Joe, wagging her hairy finger at them both.

"Of course my dear, we shall return safe and sound before you know it!" replied the General.

* * *

It was just under one hour's walk to where the Gurglewobblers launch was anchored on the beach, near the estuary of the Orchid River. The rescue party picked up all their equipment; kit bag, sandwiches and water, and were now ready to depart.

General Joe and Seth walked alongside each other leading the rescue party from the front, whilst the rest of the party followed close behind them. Every now and again Livia or Leo would stop to pick up a coloured stone or piece of jade to investigate out of curiosity. As the rays of the sun refracted on it, Leo remarked, "I can see how the Valley of the Gems got its name."

"Look at this one," exclaimed Livia picking up a tiny pebble, "it's the colour of turquoise, how beautiful, and it just happens to be my favourite colour."

"All the stones seem to reflect different colours, it's like magic or something," retorted Leo, picking up more shingle to look at, "I've never seen anything quite like it," he said.

The atmosphere within the group was now one of foreboding. They all realized that the task that lay before them was not going to be easy.

Artie and Banjo felt that they were in safe hands on this adventure with these brave little people. They would be good to have around in an emergency, as it was the first time ever that Artie and Banjo had left their own valley. But Artie's mind was quietly thinking along different lines, "What if somebody gets hurt? Or worse, it would all be my fault, phew! This would be a heavy burden to bear if it all goes pear shaped."

Rafe had gone on ahead of the rest of the party, but soon reappeared.

"The launch is not too far ahead now, General, and the coast ahead is clear," Rafe said as he turned to speak to Seth, "The sea is calm, with the occasional surf on the waves. I'm so looking forward to the boat trip. Let's hope it is plain sailing."

Rafe was feeling upbeat, it would be his first time on the high seas, and he couldn't wait. He went on ahead of the rescue party, taking long striding paces with abounding energy, wanting to be the first to arrive at the launch.

Both General Joe and Seth thanked Rafe, and continued to walk along the trail and talk together.

"Although Rafe is a lot younger than me and one can never close the gap of experience, he is a good pal and very loyal. He is so enthusiastic to learn how to do things that one can't help but admire him," said General Joe.

"It is refreshing to see that approach from the younger generation," Seth replied.

They had now arrived at the beach in the Bay of Gems, to find Rafe jubilant and raring to go. The tide was almost fully out, but they had to get across the wet beach to their motor launch, *Moana*.

Soggy boots and wet trouser bottoms were not the order of the day, so the Gurglewobblers removed their boots and rolled up their trouser legs. The Orchids and Flower people, along with the Gurglewobblers gingerly tiptoed across the wet golden sand. They enjoyed the sensation of the warm rippling sea between their toes, being careful to avoid the jagged coral and seashells that lay scattered around the seashore.

Peering out of the jet-black rock pools were rows of eager eyes from the crabs. As they basked in the sunrays they cheered these brave warriors on their way. These excitable crustaceans waved their tiny red and green banners of seaweed at them, resembling crowds gathering in the streets for the Queen's coronation.

Seth helped the girls into the boat.

"Now squeeze together as tight as you can," said Seth.

Zena took the Generals kit bag and baton off him, and placed it under the seat at the front.

"I suspect it may be necessary for you to get your hands on this en-route!" Zena declared.

The boys tossed all the shoes haphazardly into the launch, and clambered in themselves, except for Hugo. Leo had taken the flasks of water off him and clung on to them tightly with his sandwiches.

"The thought of soggy salty sandwiches, yuk!" exclaimed Leo, being careful not to drop them into the sea.

Once everybody had got comfortable, they put their boots back on. Hugo pushed the boat out then climbed aboard himself to take over at the helm, turning the wooden key in the ignition.

"Guy, we have forgotten our fishing rods!" exclaimed Hugo.

"Not to worry brother, I am sure we can borrow the Generals rod, can't we?" said Guy looking in General Joe's direction expectantly.

General Joe continued to look straight ahead at this magnificent undulating tidal blue blanket.

"Yes, that's perfectly okay!" answered General Joe,

not thinking for one moment that he was going to regret it.

As the rumble of the engine started, the tiniest of fishes poked their little noses out of the water, and waggled their tiny little fins to say goodbye.

The rescue party were at last, finally on their way. They were heading towards Orchid Sounds over the choppy sea, in a northward direction. As they departed they waved goodbye to the well wishers left on the beach.

"I might grab a takeaway of dressed crab for supper on the way home tonight," said Hugo with a cheeky smirk across his face.

"I don't think so!" retorted Livia.

Hugo knew he was only joking, but how he enjoyed teasing Livia, she fell for it every time.

* * *

Leo was feeling queasy with the rocking motion from the waves. He pulled the white handkerchief from his top pocket and dabbed his sweaty brow.

"I don't feel too good!" Leo announced.

"What's the matter?" asked Seth.

"I feel sick!" Leo replied.

"Look at the view, it will take your mind off it," retorted Seth.

"I've got an idea for Leo's seasickness," Hugo announced.

"Take over at the helm Leo. Guy, it's time to get the fishing rod out and catch something for lunch!" said Hugo, wanting to keep the sandwiches for later.

Hugo rummaged under the seat next to him, with one hand, to where General Joe was stationed. He dragged the kit bag from underneath him, tossing it over his shoulder to Guy, narrowly missing Artie, Livia and Seth.

"Be careful Hugo," cried Artie, "you could do some serious damage to my petals with that."

"Sorry!" exclaimed Hugo in retort and carried on regardless.

Leo agreed to swap seats with Hugo and clambered from the middle of the boat, trying not to step on anybody. He took over at the helm, whilst Guy dug deep to find the fishing rod in the Generals kit bag.

"Blimey General, you've got everything in here but the kitchen sink. Is all this stuff necessary?" said Guy.

"It is indeed," replied General Joe, continuing to enjoy looking at the view.

"This is my first time at sea you know. Look at that over there," the General said, pointing from the starboard side of the launch towards the small group of peaked volcanic islands. They all turned their heads to look.

"How are you feeling now Leo?" asked Livia.

"Oh, that's much better thankyou. I think I shall be alright now," Leo replied, as he clung on for dear life to the wooden steering wheel. "Mm, I rather like this," he uttered.

Roxy, Zena and Rafe were sitting at the stern of the launch, with Banjo squatting just in front of them. It was their first time on the saltwater highway too, and the fare seas motion of the launch tilted them from port to starboard. They were having a whale of a time and were happily going with the flow. Their five senses absorbed all that surrounded them, and the entertainment that was coming from the bow of the launch was keeping them amused, whilst taking in this spectacular vista.

"It's too crowded for fishing," Seth said to Guy.

"Nonsense," answered Guy, handing the fishing rod over to Hugo. Everybody had to budge up together to make room.

Hugo peeled back the lid of his little can of bait to reveal tiny ugly wriggly purbles.

"Such funny little creatures!" Hugo declared, as he picked out his intended victim. As Hugo went to place the little purble onto the hook, it made a last ditch attempt at freedom. It had to use all its strength to try and escape, landing on Rafe's lap.

"Yikes, what's that?" asked Rafe surprised, having never seen one of these before. The little creature clung on tightly to Rafe's skinny legs, knowing inevitably the end was nigh.

"That's what we call fish bait," replied Hugo, as he quickly retrieved it and put it on the hook then cast his line. Hugo sat there watching the float bob up and down in the sea. A little fish swam right up close and snatched the bait right off the line right before his eyes in one foul swoop.

"Oh, here we go!" Hugo exclaimed, "The fish thinks it is *his* feeding time. What he doesn't understand is that it is *our* feeding time," as he reeled his line back in. He delved back into his can for more bait and re-cast the line again from over his shoulder. Hugo immediately felt a sharp pricking pain piercing his flesh in his buttocks through his trousers.

"OUCH, OUCH! I'M HOOKED, OH NO!" Hugo bellowed, trying to remove the offending item from his buttock. He yanked the line and cast himself overboard. He was heading towards the ocean, head first, with his mouth wide open.

"MAN OVERBOARD!" Hugo cried, as he splashed

The Boat Trip

into the sea, bobbing up and down like a cork floating in the salty water. He came face to face with the small fish that had taken his bait. Was this little fish really splitting his sides laughing at him? Surely not! The little fish beat a hasty retreat into the deep abyss.

"Henderson turn," Guy shouted.

"Who is Henderson?" retorted Leo.

"That would be the name of the term used to manouvre the launch to pick up a survivor," answered Guy.

"Leo, turn the boat around, we have to go back for him," Seth said angrily.

"Must we, this is so typical of Hugo," retorted Leo.

Leo did as requested, and circled the boat round to pick him up. Hugo had had a saltwater mouthwash and was not feeling too good. The launch drew alongside him and Guy and Seth hauled him in.

"Watch out, I've a hook in my bottom, you know!" Hugo cried out in pain.

"You're a big fish to fry Hugo!" exclaimed Guy.

"Thanks pal. Can you get it out, please?" squealed Hugo.

"Keep still, wriggle bottom. You'll make it worse," answered Guy.

"Easy for you to say, it's not your derriere on the line," retorted Hugo sharply.

General Joe fixed his monocle over his eye socket, and turned to look with regret at the damage to Hugo's hindquarters.

"My, my, Hugo. It's like travelling with a bear with a sore head!" exclaimed the General.

"It's not my head, IT'S MY BOTTOM!" bellowed Hugo painfully.

Zena and Rafe reached over to the kit bag and

166

rummaged around in it for the first aid kit and magic tonic. They found the scissors and passed them to Guy, who snipped the line and removed the hook. Hugo then had to embarrassingly show the barest of his essentials, as Rafe leant forward to clean his wound with magic tonic.

"There is a plaster for everything," Rafe said, as he stuck one on Hugo's flesh wound, "There, that should soon be feeling better."

"Oooh! That hurts," Hugo moaned, while pulling his trousers up.

"That's you done, hook, line and sinker," stated Guy mockingly.

Hugo took a swig of the magic tonic.

"Thanks Roxy and Rafe. Strictly for medicinal purposes, you understand," said Hugo.

"That's what brothers and friends are for! Look on the bright side, you now have a fisherman's tale to tell," said Guy, chuckling. He just couldn't miss this opportunity to get one in across the bow.

"It's only a flesh wound Hugo, you'll live," Rafe said.

"Please calm down Hugo! We don't need any more accidents, do we?" Roxy piped up.

"People that live in glass houses!" exclaimed Zena looking at Roxy.

"What do you mean?" asked Roxy, glaring back at Zena, knowing full well what she was referring to.

"Well, you are a fine one to talk about accidents," retorted Zena.

General Joe was in high dudgeon.

"Now that's enough. Accidents sometimes happen," he said.

Before anyone else could open their mouths to speak, General Joe addressed the whole group.

"This is a serious mission," he said, and asked Guy to put the fishing rod back into his kit bag.

Feeling the tension of the situation, and trying to lighten the atmosphere by changing the subject, Roxy asked, "Are we nearly there?"

"Oh, here we go again," said Rafe, "you kept asking the same question over and over again when we were in the Loon balloon, just before you burst it."

"Oh, not that again!" replied Roxy, "and no I didn't."

"Yes you did," retorted Rafe.

"Now settle down both of you, we have all had enough of this foolishness," interrupted Seth. "I will tell you when we are there," he added.

Hugo was now patched up and sitting quietly behind Banjo. Everybody was now beginning to feel peckish, and there was no sushi to eat for obvious reasons. They ravenously tucked into some of the egg sandwiches with gusto, being mindful to save the crusts for later.

Rafe had just about got the hang of chewing and swallowing this new fangled food, and was rather enjoying it. As he neared the end of his fine feast and with a mouthful of sandwich said, "Look, over there, I can see the Aolian Mountains," pointing to the distant high peaks.

"Your right Rafe, lets moor the boat over there on the beach," said Seth, relieved that this part of the adventure was over, for the time being at any rate.

Leo steered a course heading for the shallow waters of the shore at the north end of the beach, just south of the Bay of Vultures.

Hugo and Guy rolled up their trouser bottoms and jumped out first into the shallow water, wetting their shoes in the sea. They pulled the boat up on to the sandy beach to enable everybody else to alight, making sure they had gathered all their belongings together. The rescue party inhaled the invigorating fresh salty sea air deep into their lungs, and sallied forth across this sandy landscape towards the forest at the edge of the beach. It was time to head in a northeasterly direction towards the Aolian foothills.

The intrepid travellers made haste whilst the sun shone. They found great pleasure from the warmth of the daystar on their backs. The shade offered by the canopy of needles from the sprackling trees was a welcome relief, coupled with the aromatic smell of spruce, was a clear reminder of the sweet smells of home.

As they walked along the trail they listened for the sounds of the busy Loonatics, scrunching the leaves and twigs underfoot with every step. After they had covered a considerable distance the rescue party reached a clearing within the forest, which Seth and General Joe agreed was the safest area for group two to make the base camp.

General Joe needed to equip Seth and his group with the spare string and survival guidebook. The book would make a great read if nothing else. The extra catapult with horse chestnuts for ammunition, could prove invaluable to group two, just in case. The General with his party would take the rest.

"Right, this is where we leave you and your group Seth. You should be quite safe here, and remember that if we are not back by dusk, you know what you have to do," said General Joe.

"We're hoping it won't come to that General, but we will be ready," replied Seth.

Seth, Leo, Livia and Roxy wished their brave companions farewell and good luck, and were looking forward to their safe return with the precious Cabbergé egg.

Livia untied one of the red ribbons in her hair, and gave it to Zena to take with her.

"Grandma Gurgle used to say that a red ribbon will bring you good luck in friendship, but I hope in this case it will bring all of you good luck on this dangerous task," she said.

"Thankyou Livia. That is really kind of you. I shall wear it with pride," Zena replied.

"I just hope it works," said Livia, as she tied the ribbon around Zena's wrist and gave her a hug goodbye.

From this vantage point, group two could still see the launch in the distance, and could keep a watchful eye on the tide. Other than that they were to lie low and stay out of sight.

Zena offered to carry General Joe's kit bag as they sallied forth together on the trail towards the foothills of Ajani Ridge in the Aolian Mountains.

As they neared the target, but still on the dusty trail, just prior to the foothills, General Joe asked Zena to find the leftover crusts from lunch in the kit bag, and give them out to Artie and Banjo.

"This is not for you to eat. It is to be used for bait to trap the thieving magpies, hopefully Cedric," said the General.

"When I give the order, I would like Rafe, Zena, Hugo and Guy to get off the trail and hide in the bushes or behind the trees. Artie and Banjo are to walk ahead of the remainder of the party, but to always keep in visual contact."

The rescue party continued on furtively. Hugo and Guy found a small branch on the ground, and as they bent over to pick it up, something dropped on Hugo's head. It was wet and warm as it trickled down his face.

"What's that?" asked Hugo, looking at Guy.

"It looks like honey or something," said Guy taking a closer look, "it's brown anyway, whatever it is."

"Must be bee droppings or similar," retorted Hugo, as he wiped the sticky residue away with his hand.

"That's meant to be a lucky sign!" declared Guy.

Artie and Banjo were way ahead by now and had heard the disturbance behind them, and had found it quite amusing. How it reminded them of themselves, but they were choosing to ignore it and carry on unhindered. They were far too busy exploring this fascinating new environment. They ran from side to side of the dusty trail, scattering the breadcrumbs far and wide across this leafy suburban avenue of tall trees. Artie had stopped to pick up a multicoloured stone to show Banjo.

"Look Banjo, see how it changes colour in the sunlight," said Artie.

"Wow, that's pretty," replied Banjo, taking the pebble from his brother for closer scrutiny.

Artie had seen something move out of the corner of his eye and gone over to investigate, leaving his brother holding the little pebble. It was a shy shickleback creeping along the edge of the trail.

"Banjo, come and look at this. Here's one of those shy thingamabobs that I was telling you about, you know, like Ickle," said Artie.

Artie bent down to gently stroke its shell with his hand. The tiny creature recoiled back, terrified, into the safe haven of its whorl.

Banjo followed Artie and bent down for a closer look.

"I've never seen one of those before," Banjo remarked.

"You know Banjo, you really should get out more often," replied Artie.

CHAPTER 20

JALEN'S FIRST MISSION

Jalen was now stirring from his midday nap. He opened his eyes and stretched his tiny wings to their maximum. As he yawned, he saw that Chad was standing by his hammock.

"It is now time for your task, little fella," Chad said softly. He handed Jalen a bowl full of his favourite fruit berry and nut sundae, "here, eat this, it will give you plenty of energy."

"Ooh, thankyou Chad," said Jalen. Jalen tucked in to this wild concoction of sweet and bitter flavours, recalling his dream that had seemed so real, like it was yesterday.

"I had a wonderful dream Chad. I dreamt that I was playing with my mother when I was tiny and she was showing me how to fly," Jalen said, smiling at the recollection. Jalen popped more and more berries and nuts into his beak, quaffing them down, like there was no tomorrow.

Chad quickly tried to changed the subject, Jalen had had far too many of these reminiscent dreams lately.

"Come on, time to get up. Cedric is waiting to talk to you," said Chad.

Once Jalen had finished his feast, he got up. He had a sick feeling in the pit of his stomach that he couldn't explain. Could it be that he ate his fruit berry and nut sundae too fast? Or was it the fear of failing on his first mission? His mind was wondering all over the place. What on earth was his task going to be, and more importantly, would he be able to carry it out successfully?

Jalen followed Chad, putting a brave face on it, to where Cedric's dirty shabby wooden table stood. Cedric was sitting in a reclining stance, claws outstretched and slouching back into his broken wooden chair. He was scoffing back his dried out stale chewy nuts with gusto.

Boyce had wandered into the cave to join them from outside, and once all together, Cedric issued Jalen with his instructions.

"We need a lookout in the forest. You are to fly from branch to branch on the treetops, staying out of sight. If you see anybody in the forest you are to whistle as a warning. It's that simple Jalen," said Cedric.

"Are you up to the challenge?" asked Boyce, "It is not that difficult, and you will not be in any danger."

"I'm ready, really I am! Yippee!" said Jalen, as the sick feeling evaporated from his innards. He was jumping up and down, unable to contain himself, squawking with excitement, not quite realizing what he might be letting himself in for.

Once Jalen had calmed down he turned to Chad and asked, "But what shall I bring Ajani? He asked me to bring him something shiny on my return."

"Now don't you go worrying yourself about that little fella. If you don't find anything shiny, I can find him a sparkling jewel from my secret stash. He will never know the difference," replied Chad.

"But he mentioned sunglasses!" exclaimed Jalen, looking worried.

"We could call him 'cool hand Luke' then, couldn't we?" answered Chad jokingly.

Cedric gave Jalen a sly twisted smile that he sometimes gave from beneath the brim of his hat.

"Are you ready then?" asked Cedric.

"Yes Cedric!" retorted Jalen with an air of confidence, "I am."

Chad waggled his wing tip at Jalen as he spoke.

"Now take it steady and don't rush. You don't want to have any accidents like Buzz, do you?" said Chad.

"No!" Jalen replied, looking up towards Chad, remembering the vision of Buzz all broken and battered on that fateful morning.

"Time to go Jalen!" declared Chad, "Come on, I'll let the rope ladder down and you can have a little practice on the rungs before you leave; but we have to be very, very quiet. We don't want to disturb the boss from his slumber, now do we?"

"Not on your life Chad," Jalen replied, not having the stomach for another one of Ajani's outbursts.

They both gingerly tiptoed passed the boss to access the rope ladder that lay on the edge of the ridge. They kept their eyes straight ahead till they got there. Just when they thought they had got away with it, Ajani opened one of his cruel beady eyes, and spoke vehemently, "What are you two up to, and where are you going?" Ajani asked.

"It is time for Jalen's first mission, sir," replied Chad, as he bent down and pulled the twine to unfurl the ladder downwards.

"Oh, I don't need that. But thanks anyway," said Jalen, choosing not to answer Ajani, and wanting to get out of there A.S.A.P.

Ajani stretched his long scrawny neck forwards right

up close to Jalen's face.

"Don't forget my shiny trinket, and remember what I said about the sunglasses," ordered Ajani.

"I'll try to remember," replied Jalen, gasping in terror, not wanting to antagonize Ajani further.

Chad had become rather fond of this cute little magpie over the past weeks, and was very protective of him.

Jalen had to focus all his concentration. He teetered on the edge of the ridge. "Can I take your skateboard with me Chad?" he asked.

"No. Not this time little fella," came the reply.

This was Jalen's first mission and he did not want to make a hash of it. He peeped over the edge of the ridge, flapped his wings furiously and took off, free as a bird. Jalen was trying to remember everything that Chad had taught him.

"WOW! LOOK AT ME!" Jalen exclaimed, feeling the breeze ruffling through his feathers.

"Ooooh, that's a long way down!" remarked Jalen to himself, as he swooped to land on a small twisted branch below the ridge. On touchdown Jalen could feel the knobbly notches between his toes, and watched the insects doing a runner. After all, they didn't want to be a tasty snack for any magpie, however small. Jalen did not look back. He flew from tree to tree, stopping to observe the avenue of leafy trees that straddled the trail that lay below him.

"The big wide world, wow, this is much more like it," Jalen said to himself, "I could actually get out of here, right now, this minute. I can smell freedom."

It was a fantastic sensation. The sweet fragrances that blew on the wind cleared his nostrils of the stench of the ridge that he had become so accustomed to. The long grass that danced in the breeze, rolled like the surf across a green sea. Jalen started to have pangs of guilt, after all Chad had been so kind to him when his mother died. He had fed and watered him and taught him everything he knew. Would Chad ever forgive him if he ran away now? Could he survive on his own? And what would his mother say?

"Oh, so many questions to answer. But I do know one thing for sure, and that is, that I don't have what it takes to be a jewel thief," Jalen thought to himself.

Jalen carried on absorbing this brave new world, trying to distract his mind from his private thoughts. The little magpie saw in the distance two small bee orchids strolling along the trail. He stayed where he was and watched them as they drew closer. They were bending down looking at something. As they stood upright they scattered something onto the ground.

"That looks like breadcrumbs. Hmmmm! I haven't had those in a long time, not since mother gave me some when I was tiny," he said, daydreaming of happier bygone times, again.

Artie looked upward and pointed with his hairy arm towards the little magpie high on the gnarled looking branch.

"Look up there Banjo, a baby magpie. Can you see him on that twisted branch?" asked Artie.

"Oh yes, I see him. Do you think he wants our breadcrumbs?" replied Banjo.

"Maybe, we have scattered the bait as instructed," retorted Artie, "Guy and Rafe said they saw a baby magpie when they were on the ridge, you remember!"

"Oh yes, I do," replied Banjo.

Both Artie and Banjo stood very still and glanced at each other, then watched the little magpie to see what he did next.

From further back General Joe gave the rescue party the order to take cover and observe.

"Stay very quiet," the General said, as all eyes were fixed on Banjo and Artie. The group deliberately kept out of sight. They were procrastinating from behind the dense undergrowth. It was just like neighbourhood watch, peeping between the parted green leaves of the foliage like a pair of curtains.

Rafe was peering over General Joe's shoulder from behind a fern, "It looks like our plan might just work, General," he said.

"It most certainly does," General Joe replied, stepping backwards awkwardly and catching his boot on a small stone. The General lost his balance and fell stem over petal on to his back, with his legs now pointing skywards. He quickly composed himself in no time at all.

"Goodness gracious me, there is always something to fall over in a forest," declared General Joe.

Jalen had swooped down on to the path and was now standing directly in front of Artie and Banjo.

"Hello, my name is Jalen," he said. "What have you got there?" he asked, pointing at the breadcrumbs, while thinking how tall the trees and plants seemed from down here.

"Breadcrumbs!" they declared, both speaking at the same time, and then introduced themselves.

"My name is Artie."

"And my name is Banjo."

"Am I seeing double? You two look the same," asked Jalen.

"Oh, we are identical twin bee orchids," they answered in unison.

"WOW! That's amazing! Does your name mean anything special?" expressed Jalen with glee.

177

"My name is the name of a musical instrument," Banjo replied.

"And Artie is short for Arthur, that's about it really. What about your name! Who are you?" asked Artie.

"Oh my name means something very special," Jalen answered proudly, and standing as tall as his little body would stretch.

"What's that then?" asked Banjo.

"Jalen means 'Bird of Light.' My mother thought it suited me," he boasted, smiling at the thought.

The rescue party were still in close quarters, eavesdropping from behind the trees. They had very quietly crept closer to the target, staying in the shadows. Artie and Banjo were doing so well in drawing information from this little bird.

"Where is your mother now?" asked Banjo.

"Oh, she died, when I was tiny," replied Jalen.

"That's very sad. We're very lucky though, our mother tells us a story before bedtime while we are having our drinking contest to see who can empty the beaker of warm pollen juice the quickest," answered Banjo.

"So who is in the lead?" asked Jalen.

"Oh, I am!" exclaimed Artie proudly, "so who looks after you now?"

"There are four magpies, Cedric, Buzz, Boyce and Chad. There is also the boss, who is a mean nasty vulture called Ajani. He rules the roost from high up on the ridge," answered Jalen innocently, "but you can't really count Buzz. He was injured in a flying accident."

Artie and Banjo could not believe their luck. This was more than they could have hoped for. They were careful not to alarm the baby magpie.

"Jalen could be very useful to us," said Artie,

whispering into Banjo's ear. Artie picked up the terrified shy shickleback from the ground, and held it in the palm of his hand.

"What's that?" asked Jalen pointing to the creature in Artie's hand, "I've never seen one of those before."

"This is a shickleback, it is one of Loon's shyest creatures. You, like Banjo should get out more often," Artie answered, putting it back down on the path.

Artie wasn't stupid; he knew exactly what he was doing, and wanted to get back to the point. Jalen looked bemused. He didn't understand Artie's comment as they continued to feed him more breadcrumbs to keep him distracted. It was obvious that Jalen was enjoying his treat, as he watched the tiny shy shickleback scurry for cover.

Suddenly there was the sound of leaves rustling and the crackling of debris underfoot. The rescue party revealed themselves from behind the trees and bushes.

Jalen looked up, startled.

"Uh!" Jalen gasped, "who are you? You made me jump!" he said, dropping the breadcrumbs out of his beak onto the ground. Jalen's little heart began beating faster and faster.

"There is no need to be frightened. We are your friends. You have nothing to fear from us," said the General, trying to put Jalen at ease.

Rafe leaned forwards and whispered into the Generals ear, "This is obviously the right bunch of culprits. All we need to do now is to find out where the genuine egg is hidden."

"I think we shall leave this to Artie and Banjo, they are doing a splendid job," retorted General Joe kindly. He stood back and listened to the little ones engage in conversation.

"You met Cedric, didn't you?" asked Jalen, looking at Artie.

"Yes, I did," replied Artie, speaking softly, not wishing to recall the outcome of his meeting that day in the forest with Cedric. He didn't need to be reminded of that one. It was a lesson in trickery that he would never forget. But here he was, practicing the same skullduggery himself.

"We would like to introduce you to all our friends. They are the nicest bunch you will ever meet," said Banjo.

General Joe, Rafe, Zena, Guy and Hugo stepped forward one by one and introduced themselves. None of the group wanted to frighten this little magpie, he knew far too much. Besides they needed him to be sure of finding out where the precious cargo was hidden.

General Joe placed his monocle back over his eye for a better look at what stood before him, "mm! Cute little fellow," he mumbled.

Jalen was beginning to feel quite nervous, and took a step in a backwards direction. His mind had started to run away with him. This orchid that called himself a General had a mighty large eye that was staring down at him. Was he really a friend?

"It's alright, really. We *are* your friends," repeated the General, trying to allay Jalen's fears, whilst still peering at him through his eyeglass.

"There are rather a lot of you," said Jalen, calming himself down. Jalen had decided that he definitely liked his new friends, and was enjoying his first expedition. He had completely forgotten what Chad and Cedric had told him to do for the warning signal.

"What shall we do now?" asked Jalen, addressing everybody.

"I know a game we could play," exclaimed General Joe.

"What's that?" asked Zena.

"Let's get off the trail and go over there," General Joe said, pointing to a clearing of lush green grass. "The game is called; Guess where the jewelled egg is hidden?" said the General.

"Oooh! that sounds like fun," said Jalen, excitedly, "I don't often get the chance to play games."

The rescue party had known exactly what General Joe was up to, so they followed him over into the clearing and stood on the soft grass.

Artie and Banjo had taken hold of Jalen's primary feathers. He stood between the two of them with his tiny wings outstretched to reach their hands. Jalen was hopping up and down from one foot to the other, yanking their small delicate arms.

"This is fun!" said Jalen, continuing to jump up and down, "Who's first?" he asked, addressing his newfound friends.

"Me!" retorted Rafe. "Is the egg on the rocky crag?"

"Oh, that's the fake one," answered Jalen, still hanging on to Artie and Banjo's arms, while continuing to look all around him at this new phenomenon.

"Is the egg inside or outside the cave?" asked the General.

"Inside!" squeaked Jalen innocently. He was having far too much fun now.

Having now got the information that they required, Zena suddenly realized that Hugo and Guy had not joined them. The pair of them had sloped off somewhere and were nowhere to be seen.

"Has anyone seen which direction Hugo and Guy went?" asked Zena, concerned.

"They can't have gone too far!" replied the General.

"Rafe and I will go and look for them General," said Zena, as she twiddled with the red ribbon on her wrist.

"Okay, but be very quiet about it!" retorted the General.

CHAPTER 21

GAZALI IS CAPTURED

"The dawn is breaking, it's early morning. The insects are singing and the birds are yawning. It's time to get up and follow this yearning. To leave this land and to go on this journey," declared Gazali, stretching his limbs as he arose from his deep slumber, then began singing.

"Oh what a glorious morning,
Oh, what a glorious day,
I've got this amazing feeling,
A fabulous egg is coming my way."

"I'm feeling very exuberant today, I can feel it in my water," said Gazali, as he strolled over to say good morning to Jupitor, and fed him his oats.

"What's the long face for Jupitor?" Gazali asked.

"I was born like it. What's your excuse?" asked Jupitor grabbing a bite to eat.

"We are going back to the Aolian Mountains today my dear friend, and we are going to reclaim that powerful jewelled egg. What do you say Jupitor, are you up for it?" asked Gazali, trying to cajole him along.

"Do I have a choice master?" asked Jupitor.

"No. Not really. So come on old boy, we are leaving," answered Gazali.

"Less of the old would be nice," retorted Jupitor.

Gazali hurriedly gathered the necessary equipment required to perform his magic and bundled it on to the back of the cart. He escorted Jupitor from his stable and harnessed him to the wagon. Together Jupitor and Gazali sped off along the gravelly trail, leaving the lush green pastures of the Mystic Mountains behind them.

It was still very early in the morning and the daystar had barely risen. They were on their way at last. They had to be at their destination, hopefully before anyone else. It was a race against time. Gazali knew deep in his heart that he had not seen the last of the Gurglewobblers, Orchids and Flower people.

"A surprise attack Jupitor, that's what's needed! A surprise attack!" stated Gazali.

The time had passed peacefully on their journey when they finally arrived at their destination. It was a great relief to both of them after the harrowing ordeal of their last performance.

Gazali tethered Jupitor to a bristly sprackling tree.

"I've noticed that the smell hasn't improved around here!" uttered Jupitor.

"There is no need to be rude." retorted Gazali.

"Why should I change the habit of a lifetime," answered Jupitor sarcastically.

Gazali unloaded his equipment and left Jupitor.

"I've got a really bad feeling about this one. I can feel it in my bones, and my master behaves like an idiotic clown," Jupitor said, glancing in Gazali's direction.

The noise in the distance that Hugo and Guy had heard was the sound of rumbling cartwheels along the stony track, and had gone to investigate.

They had hidden themselves behind a blue and red

leafy scrollop bush to see what it was, when Rafe and Zena arrived.

"What's happening?" asked Zena.

"Look! There, it's Gazali." replied Guy, pointing his finger in the direction of the horse and cart.

"We have to do something with him, NOW," said Rafe, "or he will steal our egg again."

"Zena, please will you go and tell General Joe what is happening, while we wait here to keep an eye on him. But don't frighten the magpie Jalen," asked Rafe.

"Sure, I'm on my way!" retorted Zena. She sped off back to the clearing in the forest. As she ran her garments swirled in the breeze behind her. Upon arrival at the clearing she whispered in the General's ear informing him of the situation, without alarming anyone.

No sooner had she gone, Rafe said, "Look over there, the trap net is still in place from before, we need to lure him on to it and catch him."

"But what about Gazali's magic wand and that poisoned leaf?" asked Guy, "He could kill us all with that!"

"If we break his wand in two pieces and pull the leaf off, his magic won't work," replied Rafe.

They had a strategy and were crossing their fingers that it would work.

Hugo was volunteered by Guy to lure Gazali on to the trap net, while the others took refuge behind the trees and bushes. Rafe would cut the rope, and Hugo and Gazali would both be scooped up together; it would be that simple.

"IT LOOKS LIKE IT'S ME AGAIN! I'm always the chosen one! I don't want to be in there, trapped inside with him. I have more important things on my plate," declared Hugo, always the reluctant hero.

"But you *are* a hero Hugo, and have no fear. So you are the perfect Gurglewobbler for the task," said Rafe.

Hugo stepped forward, placing both feet on to the trap net as bait.

"HELLO! COME AND GET ME!" Hugo shouted, taunting Gazali, who had been completely taken by surprise.

"What was that?" Gazali said, startled. He turned to look over his shoulder, "not you again!" he said. Gazali immediately recognized Hugo from 'the great escape' incident in the hot air balloon. He lunged straight towards him, poking him in the ribs with his magic wand.

"OUCH!" cried Hugo, "THAT HURT!"

The plan had worked and Hugo had successfully lured him onto the net.

"NOW!" Hugo shrieked at Rafe.

General Joe and Zena had arrived just at the crucial moment when Rafe cut the rope with his penknife.

Gazali didn't know what was happening, it was all so fast. *TWANG.* The trap net instantly closed around Hugo and Gazali. They found themselves suspended in mid air together, swinging to and fro.

"LET ME OUT OF HERE, NOW!" Gazali bellowed, as his bulging lip twisted with rage, but his cries fell on deaf ears.

Hugo was grappling with Gazali inside this tight ball of netting, pulling this way and that, trying to get the wand from Gazali's grasp.

"It's a dirty job, but someone's got to do it!" said Hugo.

Hugo kept slipping over, losing his footing between the gaps in the webbed trap net. A leg or an arm kept poking through here and there from both of them, as they fought tooth and nail to see who would eventually gain the upper hand.

Gazali eventually lost his balance and grip on the wand as he struggled to stand upright.

"I'VE GOT IT," shouted Hugo. Then an ear splitting *CRACK,* as the wand snapped in two.

Hugo plucked the poisoned leaf off the wand and pushed it, with the two broken pieces of wood through the gaps in the net to the ground. Gazali was now rendered powerless, and angrier than he had ever been before.

On the ground the onlookers were helpless. Guy, Zena, Rafe and the General looked upwards at this ball that was swinging like a pendulum back and forth in the breeze. Hugo appeared to be getting the situation under control, but there was still a considerable amount of noise coming from up above.

"OOOH, OUCH!" Gazali shouted angrily, "I SAID GET ME OUT OF HERE, NOW!"

"Chances of that are ZERO and NONE," shouted Guy as he watched this spectacle with relief upon his face.

Jupitor was listening to the commotion, but there was nothing he could do. After all, he was tethered to a tree, so chose to ignore his master's pleas for help.

"Well, I suppose it's a bit like shutting the stable door after the horse has bolted, and I surely wish I could. It serves him right," Jupitor uttered. He poked his snout back into his bag and carried on regardless sucking on his munchies.

"So Gazali, this is what you get for being a traitor. You can stay there until we decide what to do with you," retorted the General, "Hugo, you will have to stay inside the trap net with him to make sure he doesn't escape."

"WELL, IT LOOKS LIKE I AM UP FOR IT!"

exclaimed Hugo, now contemplating his next move.

"We are one man down now," remarked General Joe. That only left Guy, Rafe, Zena and himself.

"We cannot expect Artie and Banjo to help us. It is far too dangerous, and besides they are too small," said General Joe.

After they had regrouped without Hugo, they knew that they had to get into the cave to retrieve the precious cargo. It was fortunate for them that Jalen had known exactly where the genuine egg was hidden, and had in all innocence departed with the information.

"One of the magpies is already injured," said Rafe, "so that makes our task a lot easier."

"What to do about Ajani!" said Guy, reflecting on the escapades of their last attempt.

"The thing is, they will be expecting us to use the same idea as before, and that is too predictable. We have to use a different approach," retorted the General.

General Joe and Rafe went through the kit bag of usable weapons to see what was appropriate in his arsenal.

"What to do? What to do?" General Joe asked himself rhetorically, "We need to render Ajani incapacitated and without a leg to stand on."

* * *

Back at the clearing in the forest Artie, Banjo and Jalen were playing happily together. Jalen had asked his new friends if he could go home with them.

"I'm not cut out to be a jewel thief! YOU'VE GOT TO SAVE ME! PLEASE!" Jalen implored.

Artie and Banjo were delighted with little Jalen's request.

"But what about that vulture and the other magpies?" enquired Artie with concern.

"We will have to ask the others when they come back," Banjo replied.

Shortly afterwards the General with the rescue party reappeared from the trees, minus Hugo.

Banjo asked the General if they could take Jalen back with them and told him of their conversation.

"I don't see why not," he replied. "Five for silver, I believe, isn't it?"

"Yes it is General. Maybe Jalen would be able to help us now," said Guy.

"What do you say Jalen? Will you help us now in exchange for freedom?" asked Zena, still twiddling with the lucky red ribbon on her wrist that Livia had given her.

"Because if you don't, there is a real possibility that there won't be anything to go back to," piped up Rafe.

"But what can I do, I'm only small?" asked Jalen.

"Oh, we will think of something," replied Rafe.

Jalen went on to explain to his newfound friends that he had been sent down here as a lookout, and that the thieving magpie warriors were expecting him to return with some sort of trophy.

"I need to take something shiny back with me for Ajani. He made me promise," said Jalen nervously.

"Here, take this," retorted General Joe, as he ripped a brass button off his jacket and handed it to him.

"I don't suppose you have got some spare sunglasses instead?" asked Jalen.

"No, I'm afraid we don't wear those," answered General Joe, still peering at Jalen through his monocle.

"Oh! Okay then, the brass button will do nicely," Jalen retorted, outstretching his tiny wing to accept this shiny token. "Thankyou," he said.

They put their heads together and decided on the best possible course of action to take.

"Apart from knowing that our precious jewelled egg is hidden inside the cave, is there another way in, apart from the ridge?" General Joe asked Jalen.

"No. Not really. The only other entrance is the water gully that runs directly from the Aolian Falls into the back of the cave. But that is so narrow that even I can't get through it," answered Jalen, looking in the opposite direction. "Where's Hugo?" he enquired.

"He is guarding Gazali. You could say that he is tied up for now," answered Rafe.

After a few moments of quiet contemplation General Joe suddenly became excited. "By Jove, I've got it," he exclaimed.

The rescue party all huddled together round the General. They were all ears, as he began to explain his plan of action in a whisper.

"Firstly, I promised Artie and Banjo's mother that I would keep them out of harm's way, so they shall both stay here in the clearing. I would like you to remember these wise words, which over the years have always kept me in good stead. 'You must keep your head, while all around you are losing their's.' We now have a plan, and you all know what you have to do," said the General addressing his companions.

Within seconds the rescue party had organized themselves accordingly. "Everybody is ready General," announced Rafe.

"It is time! Let's go," General Joe replied.

CHAPTER 22

BASE CAMP

Seth, Leo, Livia and Roxy were still patiently waiting at their base camp. They had sat down on the grass and made themselves as comfortable as possible, given the circumstances.

The leaves from the blue and red scrollop bushes, together with the thick bristly needles from the sprackling trees, provided the ideal parasol from the overhead sun. The tropical heat emanating from this hot medallion had turned the air incredibly humid. So much so, that there was a real danger of death by dehydration. Keeping in the shade was their only option to reduce the risk of wilting into oblivion.

"I'm gasping for a cup of honey and nettle tea!" exclaimed Seth, producing his little pewter kettle and four wooden beakers that he had secretly stuffed deep into his pockets.

"I've got the honey, but did not bring any nettles. Fresh is best, if possible," remarked Seth.

Leo and Livia got up to stretch their legs.

"Livia and I are going for a walk. We shall see if we can find some for you. Why don't you prepare a small campfire while we are gone! We shall walk towards the beach and check on the tide and the launch, killing two birds with one stone," said Leo, as they departed.

Whilst enjoying their walk along the gravelly path, Leo and Livia were stopping to study the fertile ground beneath their feet, it was the first opportunity they had had.

Leo missed tending his vegetable and herb garden. His mind reflected back to the Forest of Bark. Had there been enough moisture from the nighttime dew to keep his precious plants alive? Were the weeds taking over? And how were Seth's bees coping without them. The Gurglewobblers all depended on the land for everything, wasting absolutely nothing. The raw organic materials always had an alternative use.

Leo and Livia went down to the beach to check that their launch was still secure, and were now making their way back along the meandering trail to rejoin Seth and Roxy.

Livia spotted what looked like nettles growing in the dense undergrowth.

"Look over there, Leo," Livia said, pointing to a dense thicket, "Are those nettles?"

"You wait here while I go and take a look," said Leo. He walked off, disappearing between the tall foliage.

"Yes, it is, I've found it," Leo shouted back to her as he plucked the tough stems into a bundle, taking care not to get stung.

The aroma from the stale musty variegated vegetation wafted through his nostrils, as he carried the nettles back to where Livia was waiting for him. "Phew, it's a bit whiffy in there!" Leo exclaimed, stepping back onto the gravelly trail.

Leo and Livia eventually rejoined Seth and Roxy at base camp. Seth had got a nice little campfire burning and was waiting for the kettle to boil. The hot glowing embers released popping cinders high into the atmosphere.

"Looks like we are just in time Seth," remarked Leo, as he handed over the bundle of nettles.

"Chop, chop, Seth, we're thirsty," said Leo.

Seth set too, pulling the leaves off the tough stems, bunging them straight into the kettle with the honey.

"A watched pot never boils," Seth would always say, as it eventually came to the bubble. "Ah, here we go!" he said, pouring the hot brew into the beakers and handing them round.

Seth gently sipped his piping hot tea, "Ah, that's better," he said as he swallowed it, "was everything alright at the launch?"

"Yes Seth, it is. But I am concerned about catching the tide for our return journey home," Leo replied.

"Mm, I know, but there is nothing we can do about it at the moment," replied Seth.

Their concern for their friends was growing too.

"Why is it taking them so long?" asked Roxy, stretching her thorny arms and yawning.

"The wait seems eternal," said Leo.

"Do you think we should go and look for them?" asked Livia.

Seth was secretly anxious too.

"I think we should stick to the strategy as planned. I know it seems like a long time, but really we don't know what they may have come up against. I am sure that the General and his team are capable of retrieving the cargo. Our instructions are to wait here. If they have not returned by dusk then we know what we have to do, don't we?" said Seth.

"We do!" came the collective reply.

To help pass the time, Livia was telling Roxy about Grandma Gurgle and her funny superstitions, as she sat down next to her.

"Is that why you gave Zena your lucky red ribbon?" asked Roxy.

"Yes it is, but I am hoping against all the odds that it will bring everybody the luck they need to retrieve our Cabbergé egg," answered Livia.

"Oh, I'm sure it will make *ALL* the difference in the world," Roxy retorted sarcastically.

"I do hope so!" exclaimed Livia, not quite understanding Roxy's remark.

CHAPTER 23

THE GRAND FINALE

Hugo was still grappling with Gazali from inside the swinging pendulum. He was desperately trying to avoid his swirling arms and legs. They were spinning wildly out of control like the sails on a windmill. Gazali was bouncing off the sides of the trapnet like an escaped pea on a conveyer belt, before whizzing downwards on a heltaskelter. Hugo reached for the twine in his pocket and fought hard to bind Gazali's kicking feet and hands together. This noisy Orchid would give them all away if he didn't shut him up soon.

Having secured Gazali's limbs, Hugo plucked a plaster from his pocket and gagged Gazali's mouth with it. Gazali's deep piercing sly eyes bulged with rage. He was at last captive, and rendered powerless.

"Okay, time to get out of here! It is polite to know when to leave. They want a hero. I'm their man," exclaimed Hugo.

Hugo had triumphed over this treacherous sorcerer, and was feeling pleased with himself. He had surely given him a run for his money. Hugo drew his penknife out of his other pocket and cut an opening in the trap net, just large enough for him to wriggle his muscular body through.

"There is an old adage Gazali. Heads, I win, tails, you

lose! You deserve everything you get for betraying your kinsmen," said Hugo, as he departed. Once his feet touched down on the ground he sealed up the gaping hole left behind him with a length of twine. Hugo then sped off down the trail in haste, and went in search of the rescue party. It was not long before they were all reunited once again to everybody's delight and surprise.

"Brilliant, we are back to full strength," said Rafe, "and I will bring you up to speed shortly Hugo."

Hugo was relieved to be back in the fold with his chums again, and together they were going to be a fighting force to be reckoned with.

"Thanks Rafe. Gazali is totally incapacitated General, and I'm glad to be of assistance once more," retorted Hugo.

"Excellent my boy, excellent!" declared General Joe.

* * *

High on the rocky ridge the magpies had heard a commotion, and were wandering why Jalen had not whistled the warning signal.

"Do you think perhaps that he may be in trouble?" Chad asked Cedric and Boyce.

"It is a possibility. Boyce, go and take a look," ordered Cedric sharply.

Ajani was as per normal preoccupied with his own self-indulgence. He was admiring the sparkling jewels and gold rings that adorned his talons, and had no idea of what was going on around him, or what was about to unfold.

Boyce swooped down to investigate and find where the appalling racket had come from.

The rescue party had spotted a thieving magpie

handkershuting down from the ridge above them. The bird then began nose-diving with the volition of a bullet from the sky. He was soaring downwards between the trees, in the hope of procuring a successful landing beside the ball of noise that was trapped inside the swinging pendant. The rescue party had dived behind the bushes in haste to get out of sight. Once Boyce had landed on terra-firma, he was immediately greeted by a rather large moving object.

"What the heck is that?" Boyce said out loud, lifting his eye patch for a better look, and staring at this orb swinging to and fro.

"Now's our chance," said Rafe.

Rafe lunged forward from behind the bushes to land directly in front of Boyce, with the others hot on his heels.

Boyce looked startled and was completely unprepared.

"What the blaze's is going on here?" Boyce exclaimed, finding himself instantly surrounded.

Hugo quickly seized the moment and ripped Boyce's eye patch off his head, binding his legs and wings together with it. Guy tore the handkershute from Boyce's back, into shreds, and gagged him unceremoniously with it. Boyce now overpowered, had completely forgotten what his Uncle Swagg had always taught him, which was to be prepared, and now it was too late.

"One for sorrow, three to go," said Hugo.

"Plus one mean vulture," added Guy.

Boyce was trying to wriggle free, but it was just impossible. As he lay there frustrated and helpless, he was thinking about how on earth he was going to break free. He was trussed up like any oven ready bird just before roasting. But he knew one thing for sure, that should he survive, his leader would probably make mince meat of him.

"Phew! dinner for Ajani. Not a chance. That idea doesn't appeal at all," Boyce thought to himself.

"That was an unexpected piece of luck. It must have something to do with Livia's lucky red ribbon," piped up Zena.

"Right, we have to get a move on, NOW, before they miss him," said Rafe.

They all agreed, "No time to waste," added the General, "this is it."

Rafe, Hugo and Guy made their way round to the far side of the rocky crag, avoiding the difficult granite obstacles in their way.

"Nice view, shame about the nasty smell!" said Guy.

Hugo was carrying the rucksack to put the egg in. They climbed up to where they could see the entrance to the cave. The trio took refuge behind a large granite boulder on arrival, to wait for the signal from Jalen. The three of them together, made up a valiant band of brothers, and were quietly confident in their abilities.

Zena, Jalen and General Joe had stayed at the base of the ridge where the rope ladder was still dangling. The General and Zena were ready to scramble up, as and when the situation required them to do so. They had agreed that they were not going to leave anything to chance, and were going to reclaim the replica egg as well from Ajani's nest.

"I'm ready," said Jalen to the General. He knew exactly what he had to do and picked up the brass button in his beak. As Jalen soared skywards, he overshot the ridge and performed a loop the loop, turning mid air, momentarily forgetting to keep his wings flapping up and down. He felt the Earth's gravitational force pulling him back down towards the ground, having to execute an emergency stop on touchdown. Jalen skidded from one leg to the other, until he came to a halt, dropping the brass button on impact to the ground near Ajani's nest.

"Hello Chad and Cedric, I'm back," Jalen exclaimed, pretending to be chirpy, as though nothing was wrong.

"Hello little fella, that was quite the landing. We were wandering where you had got to," replied Chad, "We have been concerned for your safety."

Hugo, Rafe and Guy had seen Jalen's impressive skid landing, and this was the signal they had been waiting for.

Jalen was busy keeping Cedric and Chad distracted with made up tales of his adventure, so the valiant band of brothers could sneak into the cave unnoticed.

Ajani looked up when Jalen arrived, beckoning him to come closer with Cedric and Chad.

"YOU THREE, HERE, NOW. HAVE YOU BROUGHT ME A SPARKLING FIND JALEN?" Ajani asked him, spitting his words vehemently. Ajani pushed his face up so close to Jalen's little beak, his big dark ugly black piercing eyes glared right through him like daggers.

"Yes, I have," replied Jalen, taking a step backwards. He was gasping for breath and shaking, absolutely petrified.

"WELL, WHERE IS IT?" retorted Ajani.

"There, on the ground in front of you," he said. "I found it in the long grass by the side of the trail."

"Mmmmmm! Is that it?" asked Ajani picking it up, as his temperament softened. He paused for a moment to examine the treasure. Ajani kept one eye on the button and the other eye on Jalen, giving him a skeptical glance.

"Not bad, for a first attempt, but its only brass. I much prefer gold," exclaimed Ajani, dropping it into his nest with his other prized possessions.

Out of the corner of his eye Jalen could see that the valiant trio had entered the cave.

"Well done Jalen," said Chad kindly. "I don't suppose you saw Boyce whilst you were out skylarking?"

Jalen began to feel really guilty. He knew he was about to betray Chad and his fellow magpies. Jalen really did like his new friends and wanted his new life. He realized that if he was to have half a chance of obtaining it, he was going to have to lie.

"No, I never saw Boyce at all," answered Jalen sheepishly, looking in the opposite direction.

"Where's he got too then?" asked Chad rhetorically. Chad strolled over to peer over the edge of the ridge with his beady eyes.

Zena and General Joe saw the dark shadow from Chad's head peering over the edge looking down towards them. Just in the nick of time they quickly pinned their bodies up against the granite rock face, holding their breath so as not to be seen.

"Phew, that was a close one Zena!" remarked the General.

* * *

Buzz was still fast asleep inside the cave. He was dreaming of his favourite escapist fantasy again of bars, birds and Adams Ale; still completely unaware what lay beneath him. He was known for not being the most observant bird on the rock. Whilst he was deep in the land of nod, the valiant band of brothers had crept into the entrance of the cave unnoticed. The brave trio gradually made their way stealthily through this dark cavern towards his hammock.

Rafe had his bow and rubber tipped arrows strapped over his shoulder. Guy had the stun gun in his pocket, and they all had bundles of string to use, as and when was necessary. Hugo carried his penknife deep within his pocket, and had opened the rucksack in preparation to slip the jewelled egg inside it.

"Yuk, it stinks in here!" exclaimed Rafe, trying to stop himself from gagging on the foul stench permeating through his nostrils.

They passed a fragmented mirror hanging on the wall. The broken down chair and shabby table to the left of them had the remnants of a skanky feathered feast left upon it from the night before. As they tiptoed forwards in the dim light, they could just about make out a hammock further down this dark den of iniquity. It was suspended between two walls with a snoring magpie deep in slumber.

"Could this be what hell looks like?" exclaimed Guy.

"Maybe! Who knows?" Hugo replied.

"What a horrible thought!" retorted Guy.

The valiant trio could see that underneath the hammock lay an oval shaped pile of hides. Was this the target? There was only one way to find out. All three of them got down on their hands and knees and scurried like mice on all fours underneath it. As they held their breath in anticipation, Guy gently lifted one of the corners and took a peek.

"Bingo!" he said in a whisper, turning to face his chums.

"Full house," said Rafe and Hugo together, trying to quietly control their excitement.

Buzz had heard a noise and was stirring from his beauty sleep.

"What was that?" he mumbled in a semi-conscious

state. "Who's there?" he called out.

The valiant trio looked at each other as Guy put his finger on his mouth to indicate silence, as they all held their breath.

Meanwhile, Hugo reached deep into his pockets for the string and plasters in readiness for who knows what. He handed out extra supplies to Guy and Rafe. It was a tense moment.

Buzz was now fully awake and feeling much better. He had decided that it was now time for him to get up. He outstretched his healthy wing to grab hold of his crutch that was propped up against the granite wall. Right at that precise moment the hammock tipped sideways and he fell out on to the ground.

"OUCH!" Buzz squawked. He landed on the dirt floor coming face to face immediately with the valiant trio, with a horrified expression upon his face.

"This will be a piece of cake!" Guy whispered to his chums.

"Oh no, I've heard that one before!" exclaimed Buzz. Hugo quickly gagged Buzz with the sticky plasters to stop him squawking, before he could cause a further disturbance. Rafe leapt forwards and held him down while Guy tied his legs together with the string.

Buzz recalled that that was what Cedric had said to him on that fateful morning, when they had stolen the jewelled egg. Buzz tried to wriggle free. Having one wing already in a sling, one leg in a cast, and both legs now bound up; in his condition, it just wasn't possible. He just lay their flapping his uninjured wing pointlessly in this stinking airless vacuum.

"It seems like I might get to have my open air bar after all!" Buzz thought to himself. "Even after all this, if I should recover, it is probably going to be all I'm fit for anyway."

"Two for joy," said Rafe with an ironic humour, looking at the state of Buzz, "doesn't he make a pretty picture?"

Hugo hastily bundled the precious cargo into the rucksack, and they all headed back toward the entrance of the cave.

"It is time to make our escape. We have got what we came for!" exclaimed Hugo.

Rafe and Guy followed right behind Hugo, hanging on to his every word.

The shafts of sunlight beaming through the entrance of the cave caused them to suffer temporary blindness, as they stepped forward into the bright sunshine beating down on to the ridge. As Hugo stepped forwards, he caught his shoe on a small branch. He wobbled unsteadily as he recovered himself. There was a loud CRACK. Too late, the branch was in two pieces. Hugo proceeded to trip over his feet, falling down. He dropped the bag containing the precious cargo on to the ground in front of him.

"That's torn it," exclaimed Hugo, jumping back on to his feet immediately.

The sound of the branch snapping had alerted Ajani, Chad and Cedric. They looked up and turned to see the valiant band of brothers making their escape, and these thieves had got *their* precious jewel in the bag.

Jalen was left standing on his own, not knowing quite what to do.

"The cat is surely out of the bag now!" said Jalen, under his breath.

Jalen in all this chaos had decided to make a dash for it. If he didn't go now he never would, and might miss this golden opportunity to escape to freedom.

"This is it!" declared Jalen, as he swooped back down

to where Banjo and Artie were waiting in the grassy clearing. "How proud mother would be of me," he said, feeling glad to take up this new challenge.

"STOP THEM!" Ajani squawked to Chad and Cedric.

On this cue General Joe fired the horse-chestnuts as a warning shot.

"Conker and divide!" the General bellowed.

The ammunition hurtled skywards with great velocity from his blunderbuss, hoping to hit anything that moved. The General quickly placed his weapon on the ground, knowing full well that he and Zena needed both hands to scramble up the rope ladder together. They ascended at a terrific speed and peered over the top to see chaos unfolding.

"OVER HERE!" they shouted in unison, as loud as they could.

The horse-chestnuts that the General had fired from his blunderbuss had missed all the targets. "Surprise, surprise," General Joe said, as he and Zena watched them exploding in mid air, showering the ridge with the remnants.

Ajani had been distracted by the shot from the blunderbuss and darted over to the cliff edge. Ajani was so enraged as he pecked and poked at Zena and the General with his sharp hooked beak. The pair of them ducked and dived to evade his lethal jabs. Ajani's bill chipped into the chunks of granite like a raging bull in a china shop, creating shards of what seemed like an explosive meteor shower all around them.

Meanwhile, Cedric and Chad were giving chase after Hugo, Guy and Rafe.

Rafe had stopped dead in his tracks as he began to prepare his bow and arrows in readiness to fire at Cedric. Guy immediately came to his aid, sneaking up from behind Cedric. Before Rafe could take aim, Guy instantly produced a pre-prepared lasso from his trouser pocket. He stood swirling it around and around above his head. Guy then aimed for Cedric's legs, just like a real cowboy, sweeping him off his claws. He pulled the circle of string tightly around Cedric's legs, putting him out of action within seconds.

Cedric's body slumped down on the ground. His wide brimmed black hat had fallen forwards covering his eyes, creating a temporary blackout. His wings were flapping furiously as he tried to wriggle free, but to no avail. Guy and Rafe had him in a tight corner and there was no escape.

"Three for a girl," said Guy sarcastically, looking down at Cedric, and beaming from ear to ear.

Cedric's mind was running riot. He was feeling irked by Guy's remark, "how dare he call him a girl." Cedric reflected back to his brief encounter in the forest with the bee orchid, Artie. "I'll wring his little neck when I get my wings on him, and extract orchid juice from his body and feed it to his twin brother. That'll make for a good nightcap and bedtime story!" Cedric thought.

While Guy was tackling Cedric, Hugo had jumped on Chad's back from behind.

"MY, HE'S BIG! AND LOOK AT THOSE MUSCLES!" exclaimed Hugo, "WHY ME? IT'S ALWAYS ME!"

Hugo was clinging on for dear life to the back of the bird's neck feathers, trying to pull him down. It was vital for him to avoid the sharp blades on Chad's gold amulets.

"They could do a lot of serious damage," Hugo remarked.

Chad in his rage was trying to manoeuvre both of them towards the edge of the ridge, and was attempting to throw Hugo over. Hugo with clenched hands gripped him hard, when his opponent let out a painful guttural scream. The lumbering movements of Chad's legs carried him round and round in figures of eight, as though he were performing an Indian war dance around a campfire. This experience reminded Hugo of riding a bucking bronco at the rodeo.

From the corner of his eye, Hugo could see the rucksack still on the ground. It was easy pickings.

"ESCAPE WITH THE EGG RAFE, NOW," Hugo bellowed.

Rafe hesitated, and in a split second he decided that he couldn't leave his buddy Hugo like this. He shouted to Guy who was still crouching down next to Cedric.

"GUY, HELP HUGO, WHILE I ESCAPE WITH THE EGG," bellowed Rafe.

Hugo was losing his grip on Chad. He pulled the crowbar out from between Chad's feathers and the amulet, and yanked the sweatband off this loser's head as he slowly began to slide beneath him. Chad bore his full body weight down on Hugo. Hugo was in a fix, and this brute of a bird was squashing him.

Guy immediately sprinted over to assist his twin brother, by jumping on Chad's back. This tyrannical magpie had got two of them wrestling with him now, pulling him every which way. Finally, in a moment of weakness Chad's legs gave way. He lost his balance and toppled over sideways, falling to the ground.

Hugo, now safely delivered from beneath Chad, quickly used the magpie's own sweatband to bind this villain's legs together. Everything was happening so fast.

"That's four for joy, and good riddance!" Hugo said to Chad, feeling somewhat winded, but still in good humour, "which is a joke in itself, considering the size of you."

Chad had at last been overpowered. His big beady eyes looked sorrowful now, as he flapped his wings up and down, going nowhere.

Hugo took no chances and clipped Chad's wings together with the brutes own paperclip that had a few moments ago been his crowbar.

Chad's thoughts moved on to the safety of little Jalen, but where was he? He couldn't see him anywhere as he looked all around him. Cedric was indisposed, and goodness knows what has happened to his buddy Boyce. This motley crew of creatures that had tied him up like a common criminal, would in time pay for it. Revenge would be sweet.

* * *

General Joe and Zena had been kept under siege from Ajani's lethal jabs, keeping him distracted while Rafe tried to make his escape with the egg.

Ajani had seen Rafe escaping with his precious cargo out of the corner of his dark bulging angry eyes. Ajani turned and gave chase after him.

Rafe was making a dash for it. He desperately wanted to live to fight another day. Rafe ducked and dived every which way to avoid the deadly jabs from his pursuer's lethal beak, but eventually found himself cornered, up against the granite rock face, with nowhere left to run.

General Joe and Zena took the replica egg from Ajani's nest. They quickly put it in their bag as they stepped off the rope ladder on to the flat area at the top of the ridge.

"OVER HEAR!" General Joe shouted, waving his

arms in the air like a whirligig, distracting Ajani away from Rafe.

Ajani put his brakes on, skidding to a halt and had frozen to the spot. He looked left and right, undecided which way to go. Should he go after Rafe, or stay and protect his nest full of treasures? His eyes flashed with anger as he squawked deafeningly loudly out of frustration.

"I will have my brass button back, while I'm at it!" said General Joe. The General hastily grabbed it from the nest and stuffed it into his trouser pocket.

Zena and the General contemplated for a split second taking all the jewels, but had second thoughts.

"NO, that's stealing. Lead by example!" said Zena.

Rafe quickly put the rucksack down on the ground. He was ready for this evil vulture. In a split second Rafe had loaded his bow with two rubber suckered tipped arrows together, that resembled sink plungers. He licked the suckers and took aim, firing both arrows simultaneously.

"BULLS EYE!" Rafe bellowed as he hit the target. Rafe then made his escape to safety to wait for Hugo and Guy to join him.

Ajani was blinded and looked like a deranged screwball with a couple of chopsticks sticking out of both eyes, as he spun round craning his neck.

In all the confusion Guy had not had the chance to reach for his stun gun. It was now time to seize the opportunity. Guy drew his weapon from his pocket in readiness to use.

"Lock and load!" exclaimed Guy, as he prodded Ajani with his stun gun set on full power, 'ZZZZZZ.' The powerful electronic rays knocked him sideways off his talons.

"Crane your neck if you will, we shall not be stalked," said Guy.

This huge but now defenceless creature let out an excruciating scream, as he tumbled to the ground in a helpless heap, having lost the fight, dislodging the rubber suckered arrows on impact.

Ajani lay motionless from his injuries, but his large black eyes still flickered with signs of life.

"OH NO! NOT THAT AGAIN!" Ajani cried out, recognizing the offending item before him.

Guy, wishing to be vigilant, 'ZZZZZZZ', him again with the stun gun, "just to be sure!" he said.

There was a moment of pause.

"YOU COULD HAVE KNOCKED ME OVER WITH A FEATHER," said Ajani. Too late, he had been there before, done that, and got the t-shirt. The vulture was finally knocked out, cold.

"The chances of that happening are none and zero!" exclaimed Guy, looking down on Ajani's expressionless body, grinning from ear to ear.

The rescue party had got what they came for, and now it was time to leave. These birds of a feather, although still alive, were now helpless and defenceless.

The General and Zena descended the rope ladder with their bag containing the replica egg, feeling relieved at the outcome.

The valiant band of brothers scrambled back down the north face of the mountain together, with the precious cargo that they had risked life and limb for. It was now time to rendezvous with the General and Zena by the swinging pendulum.

"PHEW! I'm glad that is over," said Rafe, as he handed the bag over for General Joe to carry. They gathered together their remaining arsenal, putting all their weapons back in the General's kit bag.

They had for the second time in as many days, collected two eggs to take back to the Valley of the Gems.

The atmosphere was so much sweeter at the base of the ridge, as the rescue party inhaled the invigorating fresh air deep into their lungs. It was such a relief to escape the foul stench from the high rocky ridge above them.

Zena pointed at the swinging pendant, "What do we do with him?" she asked.

"We will have to take him back as a prisoner," said Guy.

"But what about the magpie lying here?" asked Rafe, pointing in the direction of Boyce. Boyce was still wriggling to get free and was looking at Rafe with his bulging beady black eyes.

"Oh, I don't think he will be going anywhere in a hurry Rafe," retorted General Joe. "The next best thing to do is to find the horse and cart. We can use it to transport Gazali and the kit bag back to base camp. Then begin making our way to the launch after we have rendezvoused with the others."

It wasn't hard to find Jupitor, they could hear him grunting. The rescue party found him grazing on the succulent foliage of the trees a few yards away, and took pity on him.

"How do you fancy liberation, old boy?" asked Guy.

"Ooh, I fancy that very much," retorted Jupitor.

"Well I guess you could say that YOU have been to the ends of the earth and back, old son!" said Guy, as he loosened the harness from around Jupitor's neck.

"Peace in our time, laddie boy! Peace in our time!" said Jupitor. Now that Jupitor was loose, he galloped away along the dirt track caterwauling,

"FREEEEEEEEDOM!" quickly vanishing into a distant copse of trees.

The next question to arise was what to do with Ajani and the thieving magpies?

The Gurglewobblers, Orchids and Flower people had an ethos that all life was precious, no matter what. The rescue party decided between them that in all fairness it would be advisable to leave the villains to their own devices. They believed that the perpetrators would learn a lesson from this experience, and in future not take what doesn't belong to them.

"After all, two wrongs don't make a right," said the General, addressing his chums.

Gazali had been loaded on to the cart along with the General's kit bag. He was still tied up inside his mobile prison, but Hugo had removed his gag. He didn't want his prisoner to suffocate, and it wouldn't matter how much noise Gazali made now.

Guy picked up Gazali's broken wand, and torn off poisoned leaf from the ground. He placed them on the cart next to the spell book, and the crystal ball was put inside the General's kit bag for safekeeping.

It was now time to collect Artie and Banjo from the safety zone, not forgetting their new friend, Jalen. Hugo and Guy grabbed hold of the long handles of the cart and started to pull it to the grassy clearing, where Artie, Banjo and Jalen were waiting for them.

"We have had one for sorrow, two for joy, three for a girl and four for a boy, and you Jalen, definitely makes five for silver," said Hugo exuberantly, smiling at him.

"I suppose that makes me a little treasure then?" retorted Jalen.

"It most certainly does. You are learning fast," said Hugo beaming from ear to ear.

Banjo, Artie and Jalen being the smallest of the group, hitched a ride on the cart next to Gazali. They felt quite safe, as he couldn't hurt anyone now.

It seemed to be taking forever to reach base camp, as they absorbed the surroundings, sauntering along the avenue of trees on the gravelly trail.

The rescue party felt jubilant from their victorious victory. It had been a valiant fight from all of them collectively to retrieve this precious powerful Cabbergé egg, risking life and limb in the process.

* * *

Back at the base camp, Seth and his companions had heard the shot fired from the blunderbuss. They were all becoming very anxious as to the whereabouts and condition of their friends. Were they safe? Or could they be injured? There was no way of knowing. Dusk would soon be upon them, so Seth took the decision to go and search for them, after having gathered all their belongings together. No sooner had they decided to make their journey to the ridge, when Leo spotted the rescue party in the distance.

Roxy, Livia and Leo ran along the avenue of trees that lined the dusty trail. Their pounding feet kicked up the gritty dried out soil, like a herd of buffalos stampeding their way across the plains.

Artie, Banjo and Jalen were lifted off the cart by Roxy and Leo, and walked the small distance back to base camp together.

"We have found a new friend," said Artie, introducing Jalen to Seth, Leo, Roxy and Livia.

"We found our own treasure, just like the five pieces of silver," said Banjo.

It was a triumphant social gathering as they were reunited once again, and all equally, ultimate heroes.

"We heard the shot General and wondered if everything was alright, but decided to stay put as per your instructions and wait until dusk. As it so happens we were just about to come and look for you," said Seth, looking at the cart, "I see that this time, you have taken Gazali as a prisoner."

General Joe looked at Seth through his monocle.

"Yes, we captured him. Sorry to give you all such a fright. I'll fill you in on all the details later, but for now I think we should head for the beach, as time and tide wait for no man," General Joe exclaimed as he handed the rucksack containing the two eggs to Seth to take a peek at.

Seth opened the bag and smiled. "As sure as eggs are eggs," he said, with relief, closing the bag, "but one mustn't count ones chickens before they are hatched. Now let's go home. Our ancesters would be extremely proud of us today."

Gazali was still screeching over the indignation of his predicament, but his cries fell on deaf ears.

The sun was still glowing. The warm rays illuminated the landscape on the ground, tinting the foliage the colour of amber, copper and gold, creating the most spectacular eventide. It was the perfect end to a most theatrical day.

The Gurglewobblers arrived back at the beach and removed their shoes. They enjoyed the sensation from the warm wet sand between their toes as they walked across the corrugated plateau.

Livia and Roxy found an empty swigifig shell for Talia, as a gift from the north; she would love that.

Leo and Zena spotted an unknown species of plant

for Kiandra and Elie to experiment with, and between the pair of them, perhaps they could produce a new herbal tonic.

Banjo and Artie found and old plastic beaded purple necklace for their mother. Darva was a sucker for such gifts. Besides, it would be a permanent reminder to her of how both her sons had been so brave in the face of adversity.

Last but not least, Seth picked up a multi-coloured pebble that sparkled like a jewel for Luella. Of course, the finest jewel of all was the return of the Cabbergé egg to its rightful guardians.

Hugo and Guy were far too busy removing Gazali from the cart and dragging him aboard to be worrying about presents. Besides, they were looking forward to a fish supper or even that dressed crab that Hugo had teased Livia about earlier.

"OUCH!" Gazali cried, "careful please." How he hated the smell of the salty sea air and water wafting through his nostrils, and being exposed to the elements. This was going to be an experience he wasn't going to forget in a hurry, and Gazali had had plenty of those of late. He sat quietly in the launch feeling very sorry for himself.

"How's it come to this?" he mused.

Hugo and Guy didn't take a great deal of notice of Gazali, but once they had placed him securely aboard they set about removing the cart off the beach. They pulled it to the edge of the forest and hid it in a copse of sprackling trees.

"You never know when this might come in handy again," declared Hugo, as he and Guy made their way back down to the launch.

The waves gently lapped against the seashore

encompassing all that lay in its path. The rescue party paddled their feet and climbed aboard *Moana*, with damp trouser bottoms.

"We are going home at last," said Seth, dreaming of the Forest of Bark, and his cosy comfortable tree house. How he looked forward to tomorrow, and sliding into his own bed.

"Alas, all good things come to those who wait," said Seth.

They were now all safely aboard and settled, with Jalen sitting between Artie and Banjo. They put their shoes back on and Guy cast off, with Leo at the helm.

Jalen's fluffy feathers ruffled in the breeze like a Mexican wave.

"This is fantastic!" exclaimed Jalen. A moment of guilt suddenly swept over him. He didn't want to betray the circle of four magpies. But it was the only way he was ever going to find freedom from them, and escape the clutches of Ajani. Even Buzz wasn't that bad, for all his buffoonery he was actually quite harmless. I wonder how they are doing, and most importantly what will become of my toy box? he mused to himself. As he felt the fare seas motion rock him from side to side, he decided in his mind that there was no use crying over spilt milk. It was far too late for that now.

Hugo distracted Jalen from his line of thinking.

"Time for some fishing. Pass the rod Guy, will you?" asked Hugo.

"Sure thing brother," replied Guy as he passed the rod and can of bait from the General's kit bag over to him.

"Thanks pal," retorted Hugo as he prepared to cast the baited line.

Rafe sat right back on his seat, trying to keep well out

of the way. He didn't want the squirming wriggling purble to make a last leap of faith onto his lap again, like the last time.

"OH NO, CAREFUL HUGO!" everybody shouted in unison, as they watched with horror, hands cupping their cheeks in anticipation.

"We don't want a repeat of what happened earlier, do we?" said Seth.

Hugo was not about to forget that experience in a hurry. He knew only too well how much his buttocks had suffered, as they were still feeling very bruised and battered at the moment.

Hugo looked overboard. He observed a shoal of fish swimming to and fro in the shimmering water of the gently breaking waves near to the launch. Hugo was positive that he could see the little fish he had tried to catch earlier on in the day. It was still jumping for joy after its escape to freedom.

"Safety in numbers!" the little fish shouted at him, waving its tailfin. The silvery escapee dived into the depths of the exotic coral beneath the sea.

It didn't matter to Hugo, come hell or high water he was going to have his fish supper, and it was not too long before he had his wish.

The rescue party could see the mouth of the Orchid River in the distance and were soon anchored. They disembarked and were glad to be leaving their sea legs behind them.

Hugo and Guy released Gazali from his circular prison and untied his legs, but left his hands still bound. Rafe and Guy would escort him back to the valley.

As the rescue party crossed the sandy shore, the sea creatures from the deep were there to cheer them on.

They had waited all day for their return. It was like they knew that their whole world was in safe hands again. It was a weird but wonderful feeling to be able to carry on the daily business of survival.

Hugo chose this opportunity to tease Livia again, and plunged his hand into a rock pool and pulled out a crab.

"Look Livia, this one is already dressed," Hugo remarked.

"Hey, put me back in the water," the little crab shouted.

"Put it down Hugo. You are frightening the little creature," Livia retorted.

Hugo released the petrified crab back into the rock pool, replacing it with a bundle of fresh seaweed to have for supper that evening with his catch of the day.

They were now embarking on the last leg of their journey. The events of the day had resulted in total success. They had risked life and limb to retrieve what was rightfully theirs, and they had every reason to be feeling proud of themselves.

"Nearly there," said Seth with relief. How fantastic it felt to be back.

Back in the forest in the Valley of the Gems, the home guard were wondering how well the rescue operation had gone. Everybody was anxious for the safe return of all their companions and the valuable cargo. Their own camp had been quiet, which had been a great relief to everyone, especially Elie.

The symphony of sounds from the whispering leaves on the trees and insects gently echoed through the valley, restoring a harmonious balance to the forest once again.

Kiandra, Talia and Elie had been panning for gold, to make commemorative campaign medals for the rescue party. They were looking forward to the award ceremony and the celebrations that would follow. All the inhabitants of the forest had been patiently waiting with apprehension down by the riverbank for their friends to return.

"There they are!" shouted Kiandra to the home guard. She pointed in the direction of the trail when she saw them fast approaching.

"They have got something rather large and noisy behind them," she added. "It's Gazali, and he looks totally bedraggled in his crumpled torn singed robe. He's a real sight for sore eyes."

The home guard wanted to give them a spectacular hero's welcome.

Darva rushed forward to give Artie and Banjo a big squeeze and a hug.

"You're safe, you're safe. I've been so worried," she cried, not even noticing that there was an addition to the duo at this point.

"Welcome home General. Have you got the egg?" asked Queen Kohana.

"We have two, your Majesty, just to be sure," replied the General.

"My, my, you have been busy. That's another feather for your top pocket. And who is this, making all the noise?" she said, turning to look at the shabby creature dressed in blue.

"That, Your Majesty, is the traitor Gazali," replied General Joe.

"Is it indeed? Well, I wouldn't have recognized him, unless you'd have said so. We have the perfect home for him," she retorted.

"Are you going to introduce me to this little magpie?" Queen Kohana asked Artie, as she turned to look in Jalen's direction.

Artie looked upwards to answer the Queen, craning his neck to look at her majestic face.

"This is Jalen Your Majesty, and he is our new found friend. He had been taken from his nest by the magpies when he was tiny after his mother died, and they were training him to be a jewel thief. We could not have succeeded without his knowledge of the ridge. He helped us in exchange for freedom."

"We liberated him, Your Majesty," piped up Banjo, "he was number five in the pecking order, and that is for silver."

Banjo and Artie turned to look at Darva.

"Can he live with us mum? PLEEEASE!" the twins asked.

"Of coarse he can. We will make room for him," answered Darva.

"Thankyou for taking me under your wing," said Jalen.

"Well I don't have any of those, but you are more than welcome to take shelter under our leaves and petals," Darva replied.

Queen Kohana smiled as she spoke, "It seems these two little orchids have learned their lesson."

Queen Kohana walked towards Rafe and Guy to eye Gazali up and down.

"Take the prisoner away!" ordered the Queen.

Gazali was untied and led into the second of the two secure mines to reflect upon his past actions. How he hated being in this cold dark dank cavern. He really was stuck between a rock and a hard place now, but unfortunately for him it was not as pleasant as the one back home. Now he understood how Jupitor must have felt.

The Grand Finale

"I wonder how he is? Some friend he turned out to be, deserting me in my hour of need!" uttered Gazali.

The Queen subsequently ordered the destruction of Gazali's broken magic wand and poisoned leaf by burning. His crystal ball and spell book would be buried somewhere deep within the forest.

The defining moment had finally arrived. The precious cargo was carefully carried into the mine by Seth and General Joe, and with everybody else in tow. The rays from the evening sun beamed down through the cavity in the roof of the cave, as the egg was placed directly onto the Amrit crystal base.

"WOW, what a sight to behold!" exclaimed Seth.

"Isn't it just!" retorted the General, as they took a step back to admire this brilliant jewelled beauty in all its glory.

The incandescent beams of light refracting off the walls throughout the cave, lit this dark cavern like a bright yellow and white luminescent torch. This precious Cabbergé egg that they had all risked life and limb for was back with its partner where it belonged. The replica clutch of eggs were to be kept as decoys, 'just in case' for the future.

* * *

"Let the celebrations begin!" ordered the Queen, "I shall make the presentations of the medals outside!"

The Gurglewobblers, Orchids and Flower people exited the mine and reassembled down by the riverbank. Each member of the rescue party came forward one by one to graciously receive their medal for outstanding courage and bravery in the field. Their forefathers would be so proud of them all on *this* day, and it was going to be one to remember for all eternity.

While they were all gathered together, the General thought that now was as good a time as any for the rescue party to hand out their trinkets to the home guard.

"Hear you are Talia," said Livia, handing her the swigifig shell, with Roxy standing by her side, "we know how disappointed you were not to be able to go with us. But hope this small token will give you some idea of what lies far north of the Forest of Bark. Maybe you'll get to go one day, perhaps sooner than you think."

"Oh, I look forward to that with bated breath, and thankyou so much, both of you. I will always treasure it, it's perfect," answered Talia with a beaming smile.

Zena and Leo stepped forward next, to present Elie and Kiandra with their unknown species of plant.

"Is this for us? How thoughtful of you," said Kiandra, taking the bundle from Zena.

"Yes, it is, we thought you would appreciate its unique characteristics," said Leo.

"I've never seen one of these before. How extraordinary," replied Kiandra, giving Elie the chance of a closer look, as she gently soothed its soft purple furry leaves.

"Here you are Luella. You have not been forgotten, this is for you," said Seth, taking the pebble out of his pocket, and placing upon the palm of her bud, "it is only small, but it's beautifully formed."

"It most certainly is," she said, studying it closely, "it sparkles Seth, and look, it appears to change colour with every flicker of the light."

Darva was wondering if she had a gift to look forward to, but Artie, Banjo and Jalen were nowhere to be seen, "surely they haven't wandered off again."

Earlier on in the day once the medals had been made, the home guard had been kept busy at the Queen's request. They had been collecting wood from the forest to build a huge bonfire.

Luella, Elie and Kiandra, had been foraging in the forest for spices, fruit and berries, to make a fabulous energizing cocktail for the party tonight. As they mixed this magnificent brew together in the pot, the jumbled flavours from this sweet and sour concoction created an infusion that would set ones taste buds on fire, once it touched the tongue.

"We had better taste it to make sure it is up to scratch!" exclaimed Kiandra, as she passed a sample in the ladle to Elie and Luella to taste.

"Wow, that certainly packs a punch!" exclaimed Luella, coughing as she swallowed it down. She quickly passed the ladle over to Elie, "here, you try some," she said.

Elie took a large gulp. It would be good for her nerves. "Ooh, that's refreshing," she said as she downed another spoonful.

"Careful Elie, you don't want to overdo it, now do you?" exclaimed Kiandra.

"Purely medicinal! In for a penny, in for a pound!" retorted Elie, which was actually very brave for her.

Darva was busy coddling her egg surprise.

"What's in that Darva?" asked Luella, with Elie and Kiandra standing by her side.

"Well, if I told you that, it wouldn't be a surprise now, would it?" retorted Darva, with a wry smile across her face.

Hugo and Guy were very busy, as they gutted and cleaned the catch of the day. They wrapped it in damp leaves and placed it in the dakota campfire to roast.

Talia washed and boiled the kelp, so Hugo could extract the thick jelly like juice from it.

"This is fantastic to make candles with," said Hugo, as he came over to join her. Hugo poured this glucky substance into the moulds, placing a piece of string down the middle to make a wick, and left it to cool and set.

Leo, with Seth standing by his side, lit the bonfire. The forest instantly filled with the smell of wood smoke as it crept between the trees, penetrating the undergrowth through the valley. It spread like a ghostly calm as it engulfed all in its path.

The General and Hugo had rigged up a huge firework spectacular, with hundreds of rockets that could be launched from one central fuse, and so finally the celebrations could really begin.

The rescue party began regaling the home guard with the adventurous tales of the day, while everybody made merry.

Artie and Banjo had been back to their stem to collect their musical instruments, taking Jalen with them. Banjo had given Jalen his triangle made from twigs, tied together with twine and a matchstick to tap it with. As they joined the party Darva appeared from the marquee.

"And where have you three been?" she asked.

"Don't worry mum. Here, look, we have brought you a present," said Artie, producing the necklace, and giving to her.

"It's not my birthday," she said, taking it from him, and looking at it with delight, "Oh, that's beautiful. Mm, purple beads, my favourite and plastic too! It's absolutely perfect, thankyou very much my little darlings." She bent forward and gave them all a kiss, "now let's enjoy the party," she said, putting the necklace round her neck, "it goes with everything."

"Good move Artie," said Banjo, "we are off the hook once again."

"Come on you three, look lively, it's time to play some music. Oh, and by the way, we'll finish that bedtime story tonight before you go to sleep," said Darva, "and I believe it may just have a happy ending."

Banjo picked up his musical instrument named after himself, and started playing a lively tune.

Artie gently tapped his Loon drum with his hairy little finger, and Jalen happily joined in with the percussion. The three of them together made up a fabulous melodious trio. The rhythmical beat had everybody tapping their toes in time with the music. Jalen was having the time of his life. He had never seen anything quite like this before, and he knew he was going to like his new life. All the risks had been worth it, and how happy his mother would have been for him.

As the party was in full swing, Livia took the two ribbons from her hair and gave one to Roxy and the other to Zena.

"These are very special to me. Grandma Gurgle always said that a red ribbon would not only be useful for tying crops, but will bring good luck in friendship; and as you are both my new found friends, you shall have one each."

"Oh, thankyou, Livia," said Zena.

"But we haven't got anything to give you!" exclaimed Roxy, feeling awkward.

"It's not about that, one doesn't give to receive. It is about friends and giving because one wants to," replied Livia.

The bonfire was blazing superbly, while the band was playing a jocular tune that resonated through the valley, emphasizing their euphoria.

Guy turned to General Joe and spoke quietly to him, "So what use were those barricades going to be, when the enemy flies?"

"None whatsoever," replied the General, "but it kept the occupants of the forest busy, and took their minds off the dilemma." General Joe continued to gaze at the roaring fire. "But great for a rocket launch pad," he added, with a wry smile.

Guy left General Joe to go and give Artie his catapult to replace the one he lost last year. Guy then marched on to find his twin brother. He wandered over to the marquee where he found Hugo dishing out jugs of punch and Darva's egg surprise, and took over from him.

"Thankyou," said Hugo, "I have some supplies that I need to go and fetch." He sloped off to prepare for his practical joke.

Hugo was feeling in a devilish mood. He tied a long piece of string to a firecracker, then armed with a box of matches, sneaked up behind Guy and looped the string to his belt without him noticing. He retreated behind the marquee with the firecracker, struck the match and lit the fuse.

"This should make Guy the life and soul of the party," Hugo thought, grinning from ear to ear.

* * *

High on the thermals, Ajani and three of his magpie warriors were fast approaching their venue.

"This is our final swansong," exclaimed Ajani, feeling confident, with a smug grimace on his face.

"Is that like calling the kettle black?" retorted Chad.

"I'm prepared for anything, this time!" declared Boyce.

Just at that moment Talia looked skyward.

"LOOK, UP THERE," Talia shouted, pointing to the four silhouettes overhead, "it's Ajani and three of his magpie warriors, they are going to attack us!"

The music stopped as the whole party looked skyward, and synchronized gasping broke out.

"Oops!" Hugo gulped, as he took a step backwards. The lit firecracker exploded on the end of the string.

Guy was running for his life, with this noisy object in tow. It was going off like a gatling gun, as he headed straight towards the barricade. He brushed over the central fuse, igniting the blue touch paper as he passed it.

"OH, NO!" cried Guy, as it began to smoulder.

Guy quickly grabbed his penknife from his pocket and severed the twine, taking refuge behind a large boulder. The fuse was now *HISSING* wildly on its lethal path towards three hundred rockets, and *KA-BOOM*, as they launched skyward towards the enemy. Everybody put their fingers in their ears to deaden the sound, as the stink of burnt gunpowder permeated through the air.

"Send them a volley!" General Joe piped up.

Mortified, Ajani sounded the retreat to his thieving magpie warriors when he saw and heard the exploding crescendo from the fountain of rockets heading straight towards them.

"EEEEEEK, GULP!" screeched Ajani, as the ear splitting meteoric technicolour explosion resonated like artillery fire on the battlefield.

"Oooooooh! Aaaaaaah!" came from the onlookers on the ground, as they removed their fingers from their ears.

"Too much gunpowder, treason and plot for us!" screamed Ajani, as he and his magpie warriors beat a hasty retreat, returning home on a wing and a prayer.

"Yeah, time flies when you're having fun!" exclaimed Chad sarcastically.

"This is a firework spectacular!" exclaimed the General. "Good to see Guy giving Ajani and those thieving magpies some flak!"

There was an almighty cheer from the crowd on the ground, knowing that they had seen off their enemy.

It was time to carry on with their jubilant celebrations.

Seth leant forward and picked up Banjo's musical instrument, and began playing 'The Duelling Banjos' as Artie and Jalen joined in.

The fruit berry punch began to flow again, while Guy went to find his brother.

"Well, you could say Hugo, that that one back fired," exclaimed Guy, giving his brother a cheeky stare.

Seth handed Banjo's musical instrument back to him, and went to sit beside General Joe.

After this latest escapade, the General went over to the marquee to fetch himself and Seth a jug of punch. These two old bulldogs sat together reminiscing over old times, and exchanging stories of chivalry.

"What do you think we should do with the egg now?" asked General Joe.

"Well, they all appear to be in the same basket at the moment," replied Seth.

"We should thank our lucky stars for that," retorted the General, as a shooting star zoomed across the sky.

"Until the next time!" replied Seth.

THE END